Flash in the Attic
33 Very Short Stories

Edited by Michelle Richmond

Fiction Attic Press

CONTENTS

Introduction by Michelle Richmond · 5

Mayan Calendar by Neal Allen · 10

Rear-End Collisions by Sharon Goldberg · 13

Chibas Speaks by Steve Almond · 16

Pigs Are Intelligent by Andrew Blackman · 18

Waiting for the Electricity by Mary Byrne · 22

On the Train by EA Fow · 25

Choices by Anne Fox · 29

When It Rains on Your Birthday by Patricia Friedrich · 32

Think of Me Babe Whenever by Alan Gartenhaus · 36

Staking Claim by Vanessa Hua · 39

A to Be by Zachary Kaplan-Moss · 43

325 by Hayley Kolding · 45

Flying by C.S. Kynehart · 50

The New World by Ed Malone · 53

Stranger by R. F. Marazas · 57

The Last Record Store by Corey Mesler · 61

Black Onyx by Clare Needham   62

Movement by Timothy Norton   65

Shrine by Meg Pokrass   69

Summer Gun by Meg Pokrass   72

The Lonesome Alien by Robert Pope   74

Shape Shifter by Robert Pope   77

You and PJ and Molly and Zack by Susan Powers   81

Like Nourishment by Susan Powers   85

When It Burst by Joshua Rigsby   86

Karliski Walks by JL Schneider   90

Seaside Hitchhiker by Bob Thurber   93

Relinquishing Underwater Parallax

    Delirium by M. Kaat Toy   98

Supplemental Oxygen by Eric Scott Tryon   100

My Sister Paula by Eric Scott Tryon   103

Being Linda Marten by Katy Whittingham   106

The Informant by Susan Zurenda   109

In the Kitchen by Ilana Stanger Ross   114

Contributors   116

INTRODUCTION
Why Flash Fiction?

When *Fiction Attic: The Journal of Elegant Wit,* first went online more than a decade ago, the idea was to present great stories that would be provocative, surprising, and easy on the eyes. In those days, building a website required cobbling together thousands of lines of html code and hoping it came out right. Publishing a story online was a visually taxing enterprise, the province of the detail-oriented. Every sentence was awash in mystifying code.

At that time, most journals still required submissions in the mail, SASE and all. Almost all respectable journals were print publications, many of them produced with university backing. *Fiction Attic* was a small enterprise indeed. We couldn't offer money, prestige, or very many readers. And yet, the moment we put the word out--new journal, tiny budget, big heart, a penchant for the very short and somewhat strange--we were flooded with submissions.

Actually, "we" is a bit grandiose. *Fiction Attic* was really just one person at home in San Francisco, with a laptop, an email account, and an hour or two here and there between teaching gigs to read submissions. I began with a little help from my friends, in the vein of—"Hey, I've started this online journal, can you send me something short?"—and soon published short stories by Michelle Tea, Stephen Elliott, Steve Almond, Vanessa Hua, and Gloria Frym. Longer works included two stories by the enigmatic Jiri Kajane, and Elizabeth Harris's translation of a story by the celebrated Italian writer Mario Rigoni Stern. Kate Braverman, whose fiction I had studied in college, gamely came along for the ride, offering advice on everything from addiction to mothering to boat-burning. Adding to the melee, a gang of anonymous writers spun tales for a feature called "Quoth the Raven," and a songwriter from Texas weighed in with The Tao of Wade.

A couple of years after starting *Fiction Attic*, I had a baby, and my hours shrank even more. I couldn't find an afternoon to sit down and write a chapter of a novel, but I could find a few minutes to write—and read—flash fiction. I remember pacing back and forth in our living room in San Francisco's foggy outer avenues, with my son strapped to my chest in a Baby Bjorn, a bottle in one hand and a copy of *Sudden Fiction International* in the other. Aching with exhaustion, nervous with lack of sleep, I was very, very grateful for stories that could transport me in five pages or fewer.

But it didn't take the intricacies of html code or

the trials of motherhood to make me an admirer of the form. Just out of college, my friend and former writing professor, Allen Wier, gave me W. S. Merwin's strange and beautiful creation, *The Miner's Pale Children: A Book of Prose.* Here was the poet as fiction writer, making a sort of text I'd never read before, something surprising and strange, complex and often moving. Years later, when I came across the wonderful *anthology Flash Fiction: 72 Very Short Stories,* at a bookstore in Atlanta, I saw a connection between what Merwin had done in those prose poems and what the writers of flash fiction were doing. It had something to do with compressing language to the point that it was ready to explode. It had something to do with evoking a story more than telling it. Flash fiction relies equally on the power of suggestion and of detail. In very short stories, a world is crystallized, a moment turned inside out. As in poetry, every word, every beat, counts.

In the nineties, editors praised flash fiction for its ease of reading on the bus, on the train, in line at the DMV. It was a given that our time was limited, our lives frenzied, our patience for the written word waning. And that was before the Internet drove us all to spasms of distractibility, with its endless enticing hyperlinks sending us down endless rabbit holes. That was before we could read on our phones or tweet a serial story.

Over the years, *Fiction Attic* has had a few stops and starts. Now, the website is produced using Wordpress, and building websites is so easy anyone can do it in about as many minutes as it takes to pour and eat a bowl of cereal. With all of the pesky code hidden away, it is far easier to format longer sections of text to be read on any manner of screen. The little journal that could, then couldn't, then could again, is now a small press, open to fiction of any length. But I've never lost my love for the very short story, and so it was with great pleasure that, in 2012, I revived the contest that first ran in 2003, Flash in the Attic.

The winner that first year was Ilana Stanger-Ross, for a sad and beautiful story called "In the Kitchen," which is included here. She won a dozen doughnuts from Krispy Kreme, a $25 bookstore gift certificate, and a purple T-shirt bearing the Fiction Attic logo. She has since gone on to publish many stories and a critically acclaimed novel, *Sima's Undergarments for Women*. In addition to raising a family, she now works as a midwife.

While most of the stories came through the Flash in the Attic contest, you'll also find a few that originally ran online in the journal, including stories by Steve Almond, Vanessa Hua, and Corey Mesler. In addition, I solicited stories from Meg Pokrass, who has written enough flash fictions to fill a small bookshelf.

Among the contributors to this anthology are a trucker and a farmer, a midwife, an award-winning journalist, a bookstore owner, and the former CEO of a Fortune 20 company. It makes sense that fiction writers come from other jobs, other worlds. Writing tends to attract people with fluid sensibilities; it is not unusual to drift in and out of writing, to enjoy stints of explosive creation interspersed with long periods when life gets in the way. But somewhere in the back of the mind, the desire to write is always present.

For the purposes of this anthology, I imposed a limit of 1000 words. Longer than the stories in the groundbreaking *Flash Fiction*, which were capped at 750, and shorter than the stories in *Sudden Fiction*. 1000 seemed like a good number. Even, elegant, plenty of 0s. Plenty of room to make a scene, get people in trouble, get them out of it, or parse language one letter at a time, as Sharon Goldberg does delightfully in "Rear-End Collisions," which took second place. Enough room for the dead to visit the living on a subway bound for Brooklyn, for a father to fail to connect with his daughter, and for the sun to threaten the planet and the fragile bonds of family. Neal Allen's winning story, "The Mayan Calendar," proves that 1000 words is also enough span the history of civilization.

I would argue that flash fiction is more relevant today than ever. Not because we are impatient (although sometimes we are). Not because we are distracted (although that is often the case). Flash fiction is a wonder in that it puts the brakes on, enticing us to slow down. While the story itself may be brief, the consumption, I hope, is slow going. When there are only 1000 words on the page, there is no need to skim. When you know the story will be over very, very soon, you are less inclined to hurry it along. I hope you will not read this book in one sitting. I hope that you will read it one or two stories at a time, and that each narrative, short but in no way small, will give you reason to pause.

Michelle Richmond, 2013

MAYAN CALENDAR
by Neal Allen

first place

He was born in a round hut with sticks for walls
and dirt for a floor. Ninety years ago the revolution
was still fresh. But what did it mean to his people?
Omens had picked him to be a prophet. He laughed
when he learned that. He had no knack for the
external Gods. Heaven was inside. Outside was for
man. In the core where the sun would hang were
family and the round village in the jungle clearing. The
solar system emerged over time as spinning circles of
babble: Mercury was the church rushing around
labeling things, Venus was school and its
embellishments, and Mars the aggressive cities beyond
the jungle. Earth? He wasn't sure yet.

He was loved by his parents in Mayan. The priest befriended him in Latin, and then Spanish. At university in the capital in the late Thirties he buckled into the efficiencies of German and English, the latter for his studies in physics, the former for his girlfriend from Dresden.

His tribal memory fled a story at a time. This was the way of poverty: Climb out through other languages and let the old words die. Ever since the overweening Tower of Babel had been leveled, nothing less had been imagined by the impoverishing God.

His girlfriend spoke Spanish poorly. They met through his friend the translator who helped with her homework. God knows why they persevered. She had no ear for languages. She was as German in Mexico City as she was in Germany.

In the jungle, ambition had been unlimited. Of all that was possible, the same or more could be reached on the backs of his ancestors. Now in the city, a polymath by design, he was perplexed. He could be a physicist or a poet, stay in Mexico or go to America or Germany. How to cut through the vines? His girlfriend knew; she embraced no heaven inside or out.

They bought a round house in Dresden with three stories. The words of the newlyweds were sung in duets. On the first story they beat the rhythms of home, on the second floor whistled the melodies of work, on the third floor blended the harmonies of love, and on the roof they were silent in their observatory open to the heavens.

Over time, their languages and tunes melded, dispersed, and lost consonance. Their children toggled from Spanish to German. The language of love was shared in other homes—an Indian woman for him, a Turkish man for her. The language of work became weaponry. He invented a more powerful antiaircraft gun, but too late to save Dresden. One chilly night as he copied formulas in a warm bunker, his children and wife died arms raised and screaming in the flames.

When war and prison were done, he boarded a tanker home. In middle age the conflicting languages were silenced, and Mayan was all, no longer veiled by different words for the same things. He pumped water from the village well, and he slept in a hammock. This was Earth. All these languages, he thought, could be impediments to seeing the universality of the search, and maybe it was God's desire to keep the focus external so that the internal God—the greater God— would be unobserved.

***

"Flash fiction robs me of my fallback style — long, rhythmic sentences with parentheticals and rambling interior dialogues. I'm forced to focus precisely on plot, physical movement, and character."

-Neal Allen

REAR-END COLLISSIONS
by Sharon Goldberg

second place

It is 3:00 a.m. on Saturday and you are agonizing over last Sunday's *New York Times* Crossword Puzzle titled "Rear-End Collisions" for the sixth consecutive night. Obviously you should be asleep. Obviously you should have put the damn thing aside at least two hours ago, or better yet, torn it to shreds. But Will Shortz, the editor, the Puzzle Master de Sade, has grabbed you by the end of your Number Two pencil and won't let go. Your boyfriend Matthew, a puzzle devotee for seventeen years, gave up last Wednesday. He hated the puzzle and moved on like a normal, healthy person. Not you. You refused to be diminished, dominated, or humiliated by Mr. Shortz and his buddies Mike Nothnagel and Byron Walden, the creators of this particular mind-mangling, brain-cell sucking sinkhole.

Every week, you work the puzzle in good faith, accepting it will be challenging, confounding, and confusing. And, over the years, you've allowed Will a great deal of leeway. But this time he's crossed the line. No. Leaped over it like a seven-letter word for an African antelope.

Okay, you're no crossword expert. But you're no novice either. Your vocabulary, while not epic, is substantive. And you've learned how Will and his cadre think. No matter how they phrase a clue, if the answer is a three-letter female celebrity—Uma, Nia, Ani—you won't be fooled. If they ask for "bear" or "ursine" in Cordoba or Buenos Aries or some obscure Spanish-speaking city, the answer is always "oso." You know (duh) "czar" can also be spelled "tsar." You know "It's all downhill from here" means peak or apex or acme or whatever synonym they dredge up. And, of course, you expect every puzzle will be replete with ridiculous puns. It's true, Roman numerals and Latin phrases are not your forte, but you compensate with your knowledge of the French language and international cuisine.

Last Sunday at 11:00 p.m., as usual, you and Matthew curled up in bed, soft jazz playing in the background, and poured over the puzzle together. At midnight, Matthew fell asleep. You stared at the newsprint for another hour. Or was it two? Monday—more of the same. On Tuesday, you reached an epiphany, a transcendent moment when you grasped the deeper meaning of "rear-end collisions." The letters in some of the answers crunch up; they collide at the tail end in a crossword car crash. Clever. You'd seen this maneuver before: two or three letters in one square; abbreviations for the months of the year, for example. You were intrigued and approached the puzzle with new zeal. But you made little progress. After Matthew's abandonment on Wednesday, you were left to suffer alone on Thursday.

Yesterday, after considering the clue for 71-across for probably the seventy-first time, you experienced one of those giddy moments of crossword clarity. "Some morning fund-raisers," you discerned, were some sort of breakfasts. Aha! Pancake! But instead of ten squares for B-R-E-A-K-F-A-S-T-S, only five were provided. The letters crunched in every space. A sick, sour feeling enveloped you. Any square in any other answer, you realized, could also include any number of letters. The puzzle was impossible to solve.

So here you are at 3:00 a.m. Your animosity toward Mike and Byron and, especially, Will is growing by the minute and will soon reach its peak, apex, acme, crest, or pinnacle; although an eight-letter word is less likely to appear in one of his perverse puzzles. You picture Will torn limb from limb by an "oso" or another vicious three-lettered animal. You imagine he's been impaled on a Hattori Hanzo sword wielded by the heroine of "Kill Bill" played by an actress named U-M-A. And you swear you will never again waste one sacrosanct brain cell on the Sunday *New York Times* Crossword Puzzle.

After you finish "Rear-End Collisions."

CHIBAS SPEAKS
by Steve Almond

for Eduardo Chibas 1907-1951

August, 1951. In Havana, in a studio the width of
his arms, Chibas speaks. His voice swells with heroism.
Clustered around wooden radios the shape of
cathedral doors, listeners reach to adjust the volume.

Chibas says: Batista is a thug, the university has
become a refuge for murderers, Cuba, with her
beautiful girdle of mountains, her sea bass and garlic,
Cuba starves. In her elegant buildings, American
gangsters feast on steaks and shoot disease into our
women. Roulette wheels spin and the Arawak die.
Father Varela, with his elegant proofs, dies. Jose Marti
dies. His victorious love and turbulent appetites, dead;
moral progress fails, gives way to tailfins and murder.
All that remains of history is the gesture.

Chibas speaks and thinks not of the words (they
are always the same) but of his father. When Chibas

was a boy, his father built him a toy bridge from slats of wood. Chibas smoothed his fingers along the wood for hours, pretended to march off to work with his father, a little man in a little coat and hat.

Where is that bridge today? He wonders this even as he speaks to the poor and the hopeful of Cuba, as he laments what the island has become. There is no goodness left in this place. His father told him this.

The time has come to face the truth, Chribas says, to wake ourselves from centuries of slumber.

But something is happening. Something is happening to Chibas as he speaks; a slice of mango is falling into his mouth; like a second tongue, only sweeter. The fingers of his first lover are grazing his stomach, the glorious stink of the melacon fills the hazy studio, his father's lemony cologne, applied, with a gentle dab of the thumb, to the back of his neck. These are the minutes he wishes were a thousand years.

He has to remind himself: this is really happening. This speech, these words, the plan behind them. He has to remind himself: duty.

The address is over. In his trouser pocket, the pistol is dense and cold. What is death but the end of a bridge that connects us to childhood? What is goodness but a kind of awful bravery? Chibas thinks: Forgive me father. He alone knows what comes next.

"Chibas Speaks" appeared in Issue 10 of Fiction Attic: The Journal of Elegant Wit

PIGS ARE INTELLIGENT
by Andrew Blackman

I thought it would be different when she saw the
pig. I'd bought it back in November—miniature pigs
were popular that year, and I didn't want to leave it to
the last minute. So the pig went to live with the
Richardsons next door, and I popped over when I
could. Then, early Christmas morning, I went over
with a few bottles of their favorite wine, which they
said was unnecessary. "He's been an absolute delight,"
said Mrs. Richardson. "Such an adorable little thing.
We might even get one ourselves."

I was excited as I went back to the house, the little
pig squirming in my arms. I remembered Emily's face
when we first saw the pigs on TV back in the summer.
She'd squealed with delight and said how cute they
were. She was like a little girl again, with that spark in
her eyes of genuine excitement. She was too old now
to say, "Daddy Daddy can we have one, pleeeaaaase?,"
that phrase I'd once been so sick of but would now
give anything to hear again. In fact she'd stopped, self-

conscious, and carefully replaced the excitement on her face with the new default, a bored, seen-it-all-before look. But I'd noted the girlish excitement.

When I got back to the house I almost called out to her, but thought better of it. Didn't want to put her in a bad mood--girls need their sleep at that age. So instead I put the pig carefully down in the little pen I'd created for it in the living room, gave it some water and scraps, and went to the kitchen to start frying my special Christmas breakfast. I was so busy with the preparations that I didn't hear her come downstairs. All I heard was the shriek, soon accompanied by the squealing of the pig. "Dad!" she shouted. "There's a pig in the living room!"

I started to run to her, but then the hot fat spattered and I ran back to move the pan off the heat.

"Dad!" she shouted, more insistently, the pig squealing to match her.

"Coming!" I called, and rushed out to the hall, where I met Emily in her dressing gown, pale and tired.

"What's it doing there?" she shouted.

"It's for you," I said. "Happy Christmas." I'd imagined saying those words dozens of times before, but things had happened in the wrong order. The words died on my tongue.

"This is a joke, right?"

"No. I thought you'd like it. Remember the TV program?"

"Yeah, but you didn't have to buy it. I mean that's so typical of you, Dad. I can't enjoy anything without you going out and buying it for me."

I wanted to shout at her, slap her even, but there

were so many things I couldn't do. "I was just trying to make you happy," I said instead.

She curled her lip in disdain. "By buying a pig? Yeah, nice one Dad, that really shows you understand me."

"I thought you'd like it. Perhaps if you go and pick him up."

"I don't think so."

"He's very clean. Pigs are clean, you know, and intelligent."

"Yeah, that's what they said every five seconds on the program, Dad. I'm still not touching it. Maybe it can do my homework for me, though, if it's so intelligent." She turned and ran up the stairs. "Call me if it starts solving quadratic equations."

"I made breakfast," I shouted at her back. "Your favorite."

"I'm not hungry," she called back from the landing. A door slammed, and that was that.

A few hours later, everyone started arriving for Christmas lunch. Emily did at least get dressed and come down to meet them, but after letting herself be kissed on the cheek she retreated to the background and remained there for the rest of the morning, only speaking to answer direct questions as tersely as possible. Of course, everyone commented on the pig as soon as they walked into the living room. I'd left it there in the hope that, as Emily saw people saying how cute it was, she might decide to give it a chance. But it had the opposite effect. She stood in the hallway watching as everyone cooed at it in baby voices and held it up and remarked on how adorable the little pen was, constructed from balsa wood to look like a miniature farmyard. She stood watching as Margaret said, "Pigs are intelligent, you know. People think they're just dumb creatures who roll in mud, but really they're quite intelligent." She stood watching as everyone said exactly the same thing, one after the other, and every time they did she would smirk from the hallway.

Even so, I couldn't stop myself from glancing across at her, so often that I sometimes lost the thread of what people were saying, and forgot to offer more tea. I kept hoping to see something different, but she was always standing there, arms folded across her chest, leaning on the banister, watching us with an expression of lofty superiority, these idiots making small talk, these fools who had to buy everything. She knew better.

But then I remembered standing in the same hallway a generation earlier, thinking the same thing, and if you'd told me it was just a phase I'd have hated you for it. I didn't know what to say to her, so all I could do was look, and soon that seemed to be too much for her, because she rolled her eyes, turned her back and ran upstairs, slamming her bedroom door. There was a short silence, and I felt everyone's eyes on me, and wished I, too, could run upstairs and slam my bedroom door. Instead I sipped tea and waited for someone to speak.

"How about a nice game of Monopoly," said Margaret.

WAITING FOR THE ELECTRICITY
by Mary Byrne

I got off the boat with five other tourists. No women in black were waiting to rent us rooms or drag us off to a restaurant. Most of us had no plans or reservations, but the wily French couple had a room waiting for them at the far side of the island.

So we all tagged along with them; nobody had much energy left for anything else.

The French got the bridal suite in the old house, and the Greeks lodged the rest of us in a corridor of rooms in an unfinished jerrybuilt place with no electricity. Unlike the old dwellings that hid in hollows, this one dominated the hill, its windows and doors rattling irregularly to every sea breeze. The women still cooked on a fire in a windowless room of the old house. We learned to do our reading in daylight, and carry a torch around in the evening. The remaining rooms in the new building were occupied by men working on a station that would bring electricity to the island. They just worked and ate and ignored us. It amused the French that the Greek family were sleeping on and under the kitchen table in the old house. "Anything to make a few bob," they said.

At night, fasting snails rattled about in a huge cage beneath our windows. These had been collected by the older women who left the house just after dawn to collect them from damp hedges, loading them into big pockets in their aprons.

At breakfast, the women explained how, to avoid the heat and have grass for the animals, the family and the animals used to move up the mountains in the spring, and then further up to the summits in the summer. Now they just hung around waiting for the tourists.

A German lived year-round in his old VW van. His mangy dog barked as we passed on our way to the sea. Some of us swam, encouraged and mocked by the others. The Greek mother told us later it was dangerous to swim so early in the season.

In the evenings the German made it with the rest of us to a natural amphitheatre where we watched the sun plunge beneath the water. The French and the gays usually organized an icer with drinks. This was accompanied by pieces of squid.

In the port, a sign over a closed restaurant said, "Full English breakfast." Underneath it, "With Bacon" had been added as an afterthought.

"Is that true?" I asked our landlord.

"Not even in summer," he laughed.

We fished for langoustine on the first day of season with the men of the house. Our catch was very small. The men measured the slowly struggling things that looked like large insects. Supposed to throw back those under a certain size, they made us each a gift of a small one. Too embarrassed to refuse such a precious thing, I later hung it on the wall at home.

That evening, the Greek women asked to swap my clothes for something. They obviously thought me rich and expected me to leave stuff behind: a coat, books. I was embarrassed because there was nothing they had that I wanted.

After that conversation I arrived back in the jerrybuilt corridor and was so confused that I mistook the gays' door for mine. The blond one, Mike, was lying on one of the single beds, reading, and smiled at my mistake.

Next day the whole group walked me across the island to the boat. Mike was carrying a plastic bag. I kept asking, "What's in the bag, Mike?" He just smiled. When we got to the boat, I kissed everyone, went on board and leaned over the rail to chat. As the boat wheeled to leave, chugging loudly, Mike took a white bed sheet out of the plastic bag and they all got together and waved and waved it in the gathering wind.

ON THE TRAIN
by E.A. Fow

I saw my father on the subway yesterday. I got on at Chambers Street after a long day teaching and squeezed myself into the middle seat between a young woman absorbed in her iPod and an angry man who glared at me as I sat down. I tried to make myself small, then I closed my eyes against the rush hour. The train moved off towards Brooklyn, stopping one last time in Manhattan. I heard the doors open and close and we started to move, picking up speed, then hurtling through the darkness under the river. The train braked hard coming in to York Street, and the doors reopened and reclosed. I reopened my eyes and found the passengers opposite me had all changed; the Hispanic ladies with the stroller had turned into French tourists, and beside them was my father.

He sat there, slouched and exhausted, his eyes fluttering. He looked about fifty, an old fifty. He did not look like a New Yorker, but he didn't look like a tourist either; he had a battered computer bag propped on his knee and a work i.d. badge attached to his shirt pocket. His khakis and sport shirt looked distinctly suburban, and I wondered if he had commuted in from Long Island, perhaps, where I was raised. His beard and hair both needed a trim. That was just like him--never very conscious of how he looked, his focus always intensely directed on his work or interests. I wondered how it could be him as he'd been dead for nearly fifteen years. He'd died in another country with another wife and a second set of children, and he hadn't talked to me or my brother for at least ten years. But there he was, tired and slumped on the seat. Unexpectedly he took out a smartphone and a pair of bifocals from his shirt pocket. He awkwardly scrolled through something, perhaps work related messages or perhaps a catalog of his misdeeds, then he put the phone away and leaned back in his seat, this time allowing his eyes to close.

Now he was asleep, I wasn't so sure. Was it my father? He'd had three professions and two different families; was this simply another of his lives? His eyes moved under his lids. Perhaps he was dreaming about running out of our lives towards the ideal one he'd imagined in Australia. He had avoided paying our child support, but had he really envisaged another wife and three more children? I wanted to wake him up and ask him if he had left those children alone, too.

When I was five, not long before my parents separated, my dad took my brother and me to the miniature train park. He bought us tickets and put us on the train. The ride ended, we got off, and he gave us another set of tickets, so we rode the train again.

We were thrilled. The second ride ended, and this time he'd left a new set of tickets with the woman who opened and closed the gate. She put us back on the train, we were still thrilled, and when the train had completed another circuit, we got off. He had not returned, and he hadn't left more tickets for us. The lady at the gate was perplexed, so she put us back on the train, telling us he'd be back by the time the ride ended. He wasn't. We rode that train all afternoon. I stayed cheerful for the sake of my three-year-old brother, but when our mother showed up, her face bloodless, her hands clutching at us as she plucked us from the train, I burst into tears. My brother babbled happily and asked for an ice cream, but I couldn't help myself: "Where's Dad?" I blurted, and my mother started to cry.

My subway father shifted in his seat, his mouth falling open as he began to snore, oblivious to the stopping and starting of the train. The French tourists left the train at Jay Street, so I got and up and moved to the seat beside him for a closer look. I knew it couldn't really be him, but I was still worried. His death had brought relief and a sense of normalcy to our family. The heavy weight of abandonment had flattened us once when he left, then pushed us down again and again when he replaced first my mother and then us. We were dismissed then replaced, and then he was dead and there could be no more denigration. But what if it was just another disappearance?

He left us at the train park about a month before he left us for good. My mother didn't tell me why until I was older. It was nothing sinister, just something typical. He had seen one of his aquarium friends across the park, and he wanted to talk about buying fish. That's all he'd intended, just five minutes and then he'd go back for us, but he forgot; nothing more, nothing less. The banality of the betrayal made it worse somehow. When he returned home three hours later with a bag of fish and no children, he was surprised when my mother started shrieking.

I was staring at him when his eyes opened. I looked down quickly, but he was alarmed. He shifted in his seat, aware he'd been asleep and vulnerable, but there was no hint of recognition. As he pulled himself together, I glanced at the i.d. badge on his shirt pocket; Thomas Frazer was not my father. He was twenty years too young for a start, and I had known it wasn't him, mostly. Even if it had been, I wouldn't have said anything. He hadn't felt the need to say anything to me for a long, long time.

CHOICES
by Anne Fox

She strode the length of the beach, her caftan
billowing like a plum-colored sail. No mooring now.
She was alone.

She thought about writing again, about painting.
Her paints and easel should be here, but how to
transform on canvas the tinny salt edge of the air, and
on the lined pages of a notebook, blue gauze sky and
crackled aquamarine sea?

She looked out at the perfect half-circle of
horizon curving sun-shot beyond her. One thing she
could say for him, when she thought of him at all
now: he did agree the world was round.

Underfoot, the damp sand held the shape of her
sandals, delicate outlines in her wake implying a small
woman, not burdened. The tide rushed over the
imprints, pulled back, then crept forward again like
crab fingers, seductive, persistent—like him, she
thought, not wanting to think of him—the foam

languidly disintegrating.

She could show it in a painting, not the sequence but the moment—bubbles of exploded pearls shrunk to white, wet ash—the affair as metaphor? But how to show the rumble of waves drumming through her bones, down into her fingertips? And where to put the distant shouts of children, their calls and laughter snatched from her ears by the wind? And what could they mean now, playful and exuberant, not ever to be in her real world?

She crossed the narrow strip of sand to the boardwalk. Blue-gauze sky now gray; aquamarine turned slate. Cold chilled her to shivering. How quickly the weather had changed, so boldly, without excuse or remorse.

A café was open, the outdoor metal tables empty, white tops tracked with rust. Guard chains whined in the wind. Coffee smells, bitter black, brought back midnight.

She could paint midnight. She could not paint the smell of burnt coffee searing the air, cutting through the hum and chatter of the café last night. She remembered how his fork had rattled on the plate. She could paint the set of his jaw but not the constriction in her throat.

She could not paint the growl of chair legs against the floor when he leaped up and threw down his napkin. The napkin would emerge clearly enough on the canvas—a crumple of shadow. But not her struggle against flight.

She could easily recapture the bottles holding the dark flicker of dripping candles—the illusion of glass, seeing through it. She would have to leave out her

"no," finally slashing the silence of his demand.
   But remembering how he stalked away for the last
time, shoulders rigid, she knew there was no way at all
to paint the blunt strike of his shoe against the floor,
the slap of the trays on the tables, the polite explosion
of steamed milk into heavy glass.

WHEN IT RAINS ON YOUR BIRTHDAY
by Patricia Friedrich

When I was a little girl, no time was more anxiety-provoking than the looming arrival of my birthday. I was born in early November, one month ahead of time. After two days of uncertainty and apprehension by parents and doctors alike, I was confirmed healthy, to everyone's relief. I don't know if it rained; it didn't occur to me to ask my mother. But November is very rainy in the tropics, humidity so thick in the air it feels like a translucent curtain. So chances are it did.

Rain became one of my certainties. If you waited long enough, it came in fat, heavy drops that hurt the skin. I braved it inside my yellow galoshes and matching raincoat that my godfather had brought from the then distant and elusive United States. Lined with soft white flannel, it was like nothing I'd seen before. It closed with ingenuous metal clips that gave it character. The day I outgrew it was a sad, dark day. Maybe it even rained.

Where I come from, large birthday parties are a given. They involve great preparation, formal invitations--professionally printed if you are lucky--and elaborate cakes, with themes and matching decorations sustained by equally elaborate cardboard structures. Coconut sugar candies, wrapped in pastel-tinted tissue paper with fine fringes, are rolled by buttered hands, dipped in sprinkles, and nested in mini muffin cups.

Mothers perambulate in the parties balancing their weight on high heels and carrying silver trays full of sandwiches, stuffed breads, and fried fare. Professional waiters sometimes replace mothers and other kin; they wear black pants and white jackets and keep their poise even in the presence of dozens of dirty-handed little children. Birthdays are serious business in Brazil, almost as serious as *Carnaval*.

Three weeks before my birthday, invitations went out. My family prided itself on etiquette; if cards were hand-delivered, they couldn't be sealed. The flap of the envelope had to be tucked in. Names on the envelopes also followed strict rules even if I was turning six. No envelope was going to "Mimi" or "Tati." They went out to *Senhor e Senhora Pedro de Moraes Leite*, or other intimidating adults.

After notifications were properly dispatched, preparations began. Was there going to be a magician? A DJ? A clown? For some reason, Brazilian children in the 1970s were severely afraid of clowns, so I suspect a whole generation of party entertainers changed careers to survive. Then the food was ordered and carefully prepared by the nuns that ran the large Catholic school I attended. Each of them had a special skill in categories that ranged from ceramics to music, from dressmaking to baking. I was thankful for the comfort of their existence and the familiarity of the taste of their birthday treats.

A few days before the party, the martyrdom started; to wish for an RSVP was fruitless. If you should be so fortunate, you would get a shout out during recess as indication that someone was hoping to make it. Even an assurance of presence at an event by a Brazilian is as good as none since we never, ever say no to an invitation; we simply don't show up and later save face by claiming a sudden illness or a broken car. We can't possibly say we already have other plans. That would be rude!

So with my stomach weighed down by invisible stones, I would wait and hope and pray that the party would be a success. There would be dance, glittery striped socks inside golden sandals that went with the disco music, and carefully-chosen presents, although if they were repeats, or worse, clothes, we could never let the guests know how we really felt. That would be "double-rude!"

And then came the rain. In buckets, in cascades that washed away any chance of guests venturing outside of their homes. To be sure, no one would come, and all of that good food would go to waste, or we would take it to school day after day in our lunchboxes, hiding it from the nuns so as not to hurt their feelings, although the possibility of feasting on party food for weeks was always very enticing and almost worth the failure of the birthday party.

One hour before the event, I was a nervous wreck trying to peek through the rain to see any approaching cars; the grey, light blue and white had little chance of being spotted beyond the wall of water. So I wished for red or the unbelievable orange caravans that circulated in those days. Ten minutes to go and I lost all hope. Not a single soul or a single present would make it to the decorated ballroom rented one month in advance and embellished with balloons that had been mouth-blown one by one. At that point, I always cried a little.

And yet, as sure as rain, they would make it. I can't remember a single birthday when fewer than forty people came. They arrived in small groups, as Brazilian views of punctuality defy any outside notions of propriety. They stored their dripping umbrellas in a corner, shook their hair to get rid of some of the rain, and produced colorfully wrapped presents out of protective plastic supermarket bags. Later, to my despair, they would leave with large slabs of cake (less to take to school the following days), an act of thoughtfulness toward grandmothers or sleeping fathers that had stayed at home.

It is now 39 years since that first allegedly rainy November morning. Humid and tropical Rio de Janeiro has been replaced by semiarid Phoenix, Arizona, where nothing is more unlikely than rain. The absence of rain is now one of my only certainties. And yet, every year, as sure as no rain, my stomach still tied in knots, I worry that no guest will show up for my birthday; the pull of childhood memories is just too strong. And then, as sure as rain, they always do.

THINK OF ME BABE WHENEVER
by Alan Gartenhaus

She asks for his name without looking up. He waits for her to make eye contact. "You don't recognize me, do you?"

She raises her head and smiles. "This is our *thirtieth* reunion."

"Imagine darker hair and more of it."

Her eyes narrow. She stares. She sticks a finger in the air and twirls it. "Turn around."

He snorts as he turns with hands out to his sides. She shakes her head. "Can you give me a hint?"

"Love will keep us together."

Her eyebrows arch. "I beg your pardon."

"You know, Captain and Tennille."

Confusion appears on her face.

"It was our song."

"*You and I* had a song?"

"Yes, Claire, we did."

She touches the nametag attached to the strap of

her dress. "I'm afraid you have me at a disadvantage." She holds up her hand and waves to a couple standing behind him. They approach. She smiles, hands them nametags, tickets, and points toward the open gym doors. "You're saying we dated?" she asks the man.

"Jeez, I must really look different."

"You're sure you haven't mistaken me for someone else?"

"Of course not. You're Claire Connor. You still look terrific."

"Claire Connor O'Rourke." She points to her nametag. "My husband's inside."

"Well, jeez, I'm . . ."

"No, wait!" she says, "don't tell me!" She scrutinizes him again. "Of course!" She claps her hands, "you're Johnny Bender."

"Johnny Bender? Were you seeing Johnny Bender back then, too?"

She glances down. "Now you really do have me at a disadvantage."

His arms drop to his sides. "I'm Geo. Geo Fletcher."

"Oh my goodness, Geo, of course. How have you been?"

His smile is crooked. He pretends to mop his brow.

"Sorry. You threw me off when you said we'd dated."

"Threw you off? We dated for over a year."

"Not seriously?"

He nods. His smile fades. "I thought so."

Claire runs her finger down a list she holds. "Of course, sure! Here you are!" She hands him a nametag.

"These tickets are for the bar. Each will get you a drink. Anything you want. Alcoholic or not, your choice."

As he peels the backing from the nametag and sticks it on his chest, his smile flickers. "It was good to see you again, Claire. You know, I've often wondered what might have happened had we . . ."

"We?" she interrupts. "You and I were never actually a 'we,' were we?" She watches him fumble with the drink tickets. "Go on in, Geo" she says, smiling and pointing toward the gymnasium. "Enjoy your evening." When certain he is out of sight, she blots tears. That hadn't felt nearly as good as she'd hoped.

STAKING CLAIM
by Vanessa Hua

Years before my mother died, my sister was prepared.

Ilana arrived home one weekend, clutching two packs of Post-Its. "It's time," she said, handing me a yellow stack. She unpeeled a bright orange sticky note, and slapped it onto a pint-sized terracotta warrior that guarded the living room, a gift from our great-grandmother.

The industrious chemists at 3M invented the sticky notes to free people from the tyranny of paper clips and staples. The jaunty curl of paper wound up on all kinds of never-before-possible surfaces: in a choir book to mark various hymns, on an eyes-only memo from your department head, and on the kitchen counter, as a Dear John note. Or on your inheritance.

"Let's not worry when Mom goes," she said. "You hear about those families fighting over nothing at funerals, because there's no will. It's easier to divide it up now, when we're not so emotional."

She slapped another Post-It onto a wooden radio, the big heavy kind they made copies of at Restoration Hardware. I looked over at my mother, who curled up on the couch with a mug of green tea. The vulturing of her property did not perturb her.

"It's okay with me," she said. "Whatever you kids want to do."

Her attitude was typical. My father was killed when I was a baby. A pizza delivery truck in on-coming traffic hit a deer, flinging the buck into the windshield of my father's Buick. After that, my mother saw no use in getting in the way of what was supposed to happen. Fate interrupted the mundane.

I flicked the Post-Its like a cartoon flip-book under my thumb. It would be different if Mom were hooked up to life support, or fading away in a rest home. But she'd had us young, sometimes mistaken for a big sister when she dropped Ilana and me off at elementary school.

Now she ran her own country antiques store in Sutter Creek. She wore sleeveless tops that showed off her strong and tanned arms. When I helped her with pick-up and deliveries, she had no problems holding up her end of the oak dressers and teak armoires.

Five years earlier, I had moved from New York back to the foothills of the Sierra Nevada to finish my dissertation on Civil War folk songs. I had never been comfortable in the city, with its endless squirming crowds and heaps of garbage left for pick-up each night.

Despite the change in habitat, I had trouble writing. The chunk of fool's gold, the poster of constellations that glowed in the dark, and the wrinkled 1987 Sports Illustrated swimsuit issue in my bedroom placed me in childhood, the wrong century.

"Go ahead," I said. Ilana, three years older, had always used her head start over her little brother to her advantage. She laid down the rules, and I would hold back, trying to figure out how to catch up.

She plopped Post-Its on more than she'd be able to fit in her tiny condo, and even on items that clashed with her sleek decor. She didn't have a husband, or a house, or kids, but was already staking claim to the accessories of her future life.

Ilana was a San Francisco attorney who specialized in lawsuits to prevent what could happen. She came home rarely enough to make her visits a production--ones that justified my mother cooking my sister's favorite biscuits, each time--but often enough to avoid guilt.

Soon, the living room looked as if a flock of monarch butterflies had touched down, the orange notes fluttering at times in the hot breeze. I held off. There wasn't much I wanted, wasn't much I could see in my future. But that afternoon, I hid what mattered in the crawl space of the garage, under a crate of encyclopedias and a pile of wooden tennis racquets.

The next morning, the camera I'd stashed was sitting in the coffee table, tagged with an orange Post-It. I cradled the Rollieflex in my right hand. I'd found my grandfather's camera when I was a teenager.

Its twin lenses looked liked an odd pair of spectacles mounted on the rectangular case, which rested on the small end. The camera had a large square viewfinder on top. People couldn't tell when you were taking a picture.

She's done it again, I thought. Taken what I wanted, without even knowing, without spite. Ilana had the present and the future all wrapped up. I only had the past.

"I was looking for my old cheerleading uniform in the garage, and found this," Ilana said, sweeping the Rollie away from me.

"Don't you think it will make a cool decoration, for when I get a guest bedroom? I wonder if it works."

"It does," I said, tugging it away.

"You'll have to show me how. Maybe I'll take it now, instead of waiting," she trailed off, even she unable to say, "when Mom dies."

I considered Solomon's choice, and let the camera slip out of my fingers.

The lenses shattered against the tile floor, and a large crack shot through the case, over-exposing the photos I'd taken of bleary newlyweds stumbling out of a B&B, of my unsuspecting mother, beautiful, at the shop counter, of a gold mine tower silhouetted at sunset.

We stared down at the smashed pieces.

"Ouch," Ilana said. "Then again, I just got a digital camera, so maybe I didn't need more junk to clutter up my place."

I picked up the Rollie and looked through the viewfinder: nothing. Nothing plus me.

This story originally appeared in Issue 5 of Fiction Attic: The Journal of Elegant Wit.

A TO B
by Zachary Kaplan-Moss

I sat in the camper and thought about how Annie and Brian would one day meet, perhaps seek each other out, bonding over how they're both kind of lonely and alone in the military, each a little smarter, a little more melancholy than the rest, but dutiful souls nonetheless.

They would talk about me at first. Sharing memories and thinking about times gone past. Or maybe they wouldn't talk about me at all, but I'd be on their minds. Lingering in the background after a short barrage of questions and answers: "How's he doing?" and, "Oh, I'm sorry to hear that."

Then they'd move on to other things: what they've learned and where they've been. And how they feel like the other is the only one who can really get them, the only one who can span that strange divide between Oberlin College and the Army. They're both so good looking too, so fit and athletic and dying for some company.

I'd promised her that I'd be at her wedding when we meant something else by it. But I'll stand there with a plastered sneer as my gift, mustering up an imperceptibly bitter toast about how much I love them both and how good it is that they found each other in this hard cruel world.

And then I'll go back to whatever new hole I've dug for myself in the ground. Lusting after falling flowers and spending my nights alone.

325
by Hayley Kolding

The sun was relentless. It beat through the tinted SUV windows, baking the air-conditioned interior to a neat 325 degrees Fahrenheit. Sitting at the stoplight, Orla held her hands above the dashboard fan; Charlotte, in the backseat, fixed her melting eyes on the little puddles of sweat left behind on the steering wheel. The car was awkwardly quiet. Orla had tried and failed to beat the stoplight, speeding ahead when the yellow globe lit up but not quite outpacing its implosion into the red. Her husband, John, was now staring pointedly at the traffic light. He had told Orla to heed the light's warning—"Yellow means slow, babe"—but his eyes, reflecting the red burn-out, made her wish she had gone faster.

The sound of the fan baked their ears; the seatbelt warning indicator on Orla's seat beeped like the timer on an oven.

"Charlotte," John asked, "Did you read that story

about the sun?"

Charlotte looked away from the sweat-marked wheel. "The one in the *Geographic*?"

John nodded. "It's crazy. They say that next year we're due for the biggest solar flare on record. A doozy. If it wipes out enough of the transformers, we'll be out of power for months."

The light had just changed. Orla pushed her foot too hard on the pedal.

"Powerless?" she asked in alarm. "Is that even possible today?"

"If the flare has enough energy to knock out that many transformers, there won't be anything to do about it. Online databases—credit cards, medical records—they'll all be wiped out, too."

Charlotte smiled. "No cell phones."

Her mother blinked, except it wasn't really a blink—she held her eyelids closed for a moment too long.

"Stop it," she said. "I hate hearing all these doomsday stories."

"It's not a doomsday story," John insisted. "It was in the *Geographic*."

Orla shook her head in frustration. "Then we should at least prepare for it, John. Build a fallout shelter, an outhouse, something. Start hoarding canned foods."

"Toilet paper," John told her. "All you'd really need to stock up on is toilet paper."

But that night he clipped coupons alongside his wife, coupons for canned soup and peaches.

The next day they took the grocery market by storm: Orla in cured leather boots, smelling of the anti-wrinkle cream that she couldn't wear in direct sunlight; John with coupons rustling in his pockets. His teeth were stained red from the pomegranate juice Orla sometimes made him drink. It was too bitter for him but she said he needed the antioxidants. Looking up at his bloody smile in the round saucer of the security mirror by the automatic doors, John regretted the juice already. But supposedly it would pay off Someday, just like Orla's anti-wrinkle cream. At age eighty, they'd be ready to sit in the sun, she a little smoother, he full of anti-oxidants.

Except maybe for the solar flare. Regardless, he'd been sure to clip coupons for pomegranate juice.

Charlotte had not clipped coupons. While John and Orla swarmed the canned-goods section like heat-stricken ants, she lingered outside in the parking lot. A plastic greenhouse had been erected in one sunny corner, its roof and windows misty from the humid air inside. Charlotte pulled aside the plastic curtain on the doorway and felt the moist atmosphere wash over her like hot breath. She wandered for a while amongst the plants, pausing every so often to exhale above green leaves and to inhale what they gave back to her.

In the middle of the greenhouse was a crocus plant. Charlotte pulled its purple blossoms toward her face, breathed in. The scent was ripe with the sweetness of a berry on the verge of rotting. Charlotte pictured the cells in her nostrils dancing around maypoles in its honor.

Her phone rang.

It was Orla, of course. Orla, demanding that Charlotte join in the stockpiling efforts.

Her daughter, skin damp and sweet from the greenhouse, spoke into the receiver: "I found a really pretty flower. Can we buy it?"

Orla, on the other end, breathed out through her teeth. "Buy some cucumbers if you want to grow something—something we can preserve."

There was a staticky burst through the phone—someone talking on Orla's side of the conversation—then Charlotte heard Orla saying, "No, we'll charge it, thank you." More static. Then she hung up.

Charlotte dreamt that she was growing on a vine. Her skin was green; she felt sunlight turning to sugar in her veins. She liked the taste of dirt and sunshine, and the way little winged bugs kept lighting on her vine. Then out from nowhere loomed Orla's hand, giant and smelling of anti-wrinkle cream. The long fingers seized Charlotte and pushed her into a jar of brine. She tried to yell, "I'm no cucumber!," but as vinegar flooded her mouth, she stopped to hold her breath.

In rapid time her skin turned withered and wrinkly; her lips puckered into a permanent closure. The jar was dark, cold like a cellar. Charlotte floated amidst the other pickles—John, Orla herself, and also the collie, Richard, and Charlotte's cousins and uncles. She floated there and wondered why she couldn't taste the vinegar.

Then the sun flared, cracking the glass jar. As vinegar spilled across the floor, the pickles ignited. Right in the middle of the puddle, they burnt to a pile of blackened crisps.

"That would never happen," Orla reassured her the next morning. "Pickles last forever."

Inspired, Orla led them back to the grocery store to stock up on kosher dills. Also black beans, dried fruit, beef jerky. John pulled a watermelon into the cart, but Orla pushed it aside angrily.

"You can't can a watermelon."

John, frowning, said nothing.

Back in the car, the temperature kept climbing. 325 degrees Fahrenheit, the temperature you cook a goose at. Charlotte watched the grocery store disappearing behind them. Somehow the sun-baked storefront had felt cooler than the air-conditioned SUV. She pictured thirsty pickles crumbling in the inferno.

"You should've bought the watermelon."

FLYING
by C.S. Kynehart

The dead bird sat at the side of the road. I was on
my way to see you when I saw it.

Its body was slightly crushed on one side, the dark
grey feathers pulling growing stretching into lighter
pale cloud grey. Those feathers were bent, scraggly,
dead. Not pretty. The belly of the thing was pure white
and still soft to touch. The feet, well there was only
one and a half really, all bony and thick and a grainy
yellow brown shade. Its head was so lovely, Al,
perfectly oval and strange like a baby's head, soft as
soft can be, and the little beady eyes asking for
retribution. Black like it is when you see an old road
gone over with new pitch, thinking where am I now?
Oh, right.

So I picked up this little bird. I poked that soft
belly with one finger, and lifted the flat, arcing wing.
The feathers on that wing were pristine, all arranged
just so like only God could do. I dragged it off into the

dirt, and dug a hole by that big oak tree. You know that sharp curve in the road, and the big oak tree sitting by itself? With the farmer's cows munching on the grass behind the fence, staring. They were staring at me, too, not just the tree now, staring at the new entertainment. Their big blank eyes looked up at me as I dug a hole, more like kicked around with my shoe, and laid the bird in it.

I'm sorry I missed your show. I missed that bus down into the bright light speed of the city, all that ecstasy and rush and the hush that meets you before your fingers glide over the strings. I'm sorry I missed your screaming, your lovely lilt turned into a shrieking dream and then the guitar tears up the whole room until it's just heads. People's heads rolling and laughing and shaking and nodding, as you're tearing everything up. You're tearing up the walls, too, into splinters. You're making the drunks stumble harder and maybe the little gal strumming herself outside the door with some stranger even looks in the doorway and lives, for a second. You make her live for a second.

You probably wondered where I was, I'm sorry. Did you wonder while you were shrieking, maybe, or while your boots scuffed the floor, or while you found that gal outside the door and dragged her into your dressing room, while all the heads reassembled themselves into pillars of flesh and the drunks dragged themselves away?

You made me live for a second, a long time ago, but then I went to a funeral. I went to one, and then another, and then there was the dead bird. I wonder if its mate misses it. If he cries and says, what happened? Where is she? I bet the bird was just minding its business, just like me, and then the world went and betrayed her. Just like you. You're not the world though, Al. You're just a man. I'm not going to stick around to remind you of that.

THE NEW WORLD
by Edmund Malone

Ladies and Gentlemen of St. Mary's City Mission, may I welcome you to the inaugural tour of Kim's New World. Let me say that I, and even the ex-lambikins, Kim, have a soft spot for the homeless, or, my apologies, perhaps the more PC term these days is "disenfranchised." Regardless, make yourselves at home. Please don't feel the need to wipe your shoes—or bare feet—as you will notice I'm holding the doormat. Why? you may ask. Call it a post-modern expression of the self, with perhaps a dash of self-loathing nihilism mixed in, with a sprig of ole timey cynicism and a healthy dose of Swedish death metal sentiment. You see, my patient wanderers of the urban apocalypse, *I* am the doormat. The doormat over which Kim has passed from the Old World to the New.

I'm sorry, sir. You belched a question?

Oh, yes. The free beer. Toward the end of the

tour we will adjourn to the kitchen, and if the snookums, Kim, has not changed too much in her New World, there will be copious amounts of Bud Light in the fridge.

Yes, precisely, sir. Lots o' fucking beer.

As I was saying, I am like your England to America, Spain to Mexico, or Portugal to Brazil. She has sailed from the mother country, *sans moi,* to the greener shores of this lovely colonial, outside of which is a bird bath under which is a spare key—another habit of her days in the Old World, which, incidentally, is a place we will *not* be visiting.

Now let us move into the living room. You will notice the furniture. Lovely, isn't it? The sofa here? Three more installments and I'll have it paid for.

You, madam, in back, with the shopping bags, those crusty boots must make your feet tired. Feel free to relax there on the sofa. Stretch out those legs.

It is in here, everyone, that I have set up the exhibits. They are in reverse chronology. This photograph is dated December 25th, Christmas. This is me, here, and, this is the angel of my heart, Kim, her mother, brother and sister, too. This next photo is Thanksgiving. Also, sweet Kimberly, yours truly, and her clan of gypsies. Moving on, the last exhibit is dated October 22nd. You see the official stamp of the County Recorder's Office? This is a copy of the deed to this abode—The New World, a place I was not invited to, did not know existed. See, Kim sailed in the night while I was away on business, but up until her clandestine disappearance had enjoyed the fruits of our love while preparing this shore for her landing: walks on the beach together, credit card-straining dinners downtown, and oral machinations to which she rolled and purred like an intoxicated kitty buried in a mound of catnip.

And, ma'am, there on the couch. If you can fit that lamp into one of your bags, knock yourself out.

Now, we are in the bedroom. On the bed I have arranged for you ladies a lovely selection of *clean* and folded women's underwear. Feel free to use the bathroom behind you to try anything on. Please, however, do not drop your used articles on the floor; stuff them, instead, into the dresser over here. Kim and her new beau are very tidy.

And anyone smoking who hasn't already ground out their cigarettes into the carpet, please extinguish the butts in the vase that man in the corner is urinating into.

Gentlemen, I've also arranged gifts for you, too. In the same dresser are Greg's things, but please wait till the ladies, here, are finished in the bathroom. And in the closet on my left is a brand new set of Nike golf clubs; they would make a wonderful addition to the window dressing of the pawnshop down the street from the mission.

But, please, everyone, do not touch the bed. I have a special treat for Kim and Greg when they tuck in under the covers tonight.

This is the end of the tour, the kitchen. I see the gentleman there has already found the beer. And a chicken leg, too. Excellent. We'll have a picnic. Oh, and check the freezer. There should be a cache of Chunky Monkey in there.

And anyone needing to make a call, the phone's over on the wall. I believe you, sir…no, not you, the man with the swastika on his forehead, yes, you mentioned a brother stationed in South Korea. Take all the time you need.

Any questions?

Yes, the man with the Jack Daniels.

Ah, a keen observer you are, sir. Yes, the cat bowl, but no cat. Hmmm. Can you recall the scene in *The Godfather* with the movie producer and the horse's head?

STRANGERS
by Robert Marazas

This is how it will play out.

I'll be sitting in the Axton County mall on one of those hard, uncomfortable benches, a sack of paperbacks next to me, buy four, get the fifth free. I won't register it as she walks by, because it's been years, and I don't quite recognize her. But she'll turn back to look, and stop, and come forward. Then I'll notice her. Recognition will come slowly, seeing the little girl behind the thinner, stringy hair, the puffy face (a drinker?), and the chunky body, as if her baby fat returned in her thirties. My estranged daughter.

I'll set my poker face, unreachable, bored, and disinterested. I'll concentrate on making my voice cold, distant and monotone.

How are you, she'll say.

Fine, I'll say.

I won't mention the open-heart surgery and how

it changed my life, won't even joke about showing her the zipper down my chest. She'll ask about her brother, annoying me, but I won't let her know that. I'll give her my cynical half smile. Why would you care, I'll say, you hate him, isn't that what you wrote in your diary, what is it, you want to know if he's doing well so you can wish him bad luck? He told me a long time ago if I ever saw you again, never to tell you anything about him.

She'll be angry about that but for some reason unwilling or unable to walk away. She'll tell me I should be happy about this, she's divorced now, it didn't work out.

And with a flash of the old familiar defiance she'll say, You never liked him.

Liked him?, I'll say. I didn't know him because you never gave us the chance. I don't even remember his name. Except for the fact that he had no social skills and made you drive in snowstorms to see him and then never even called to see if you got home safe, he wasn't even a blip on my radar screen. He was a stranger, like you.

She'll be wary now because she heard the pitch of my voice rise, suspecting that I'm getting emotional and start to berate her. But I'll stay calm and let the silence string out like her nerves. She'll look around.

Where's Mom? she'll ask.

Not here, I'll answer.

She's at home? she'll ask, puzzled that her parents wouldn't be out together.

I'll pause until she starts to shift from one foot to the other.

She died last year, I'll say.

I'll savor the change of expressions on her face: disbelief, horror, anger, perhaps a touch of sadness?

As the anger drowns out the other expressions, she'll demand to know why no one told her. I'll feign surprise.

For what?, I'll say. You hated her. She died knowing you hated her. You don't deserve to know anything about this family you wrecked.

My bland face and voice will sting her more than anything else.

I didn't hate her! she'll insist.

How interesting, I'll say, and stifle a yawn.

But you must hate me, she'll say.

Now I will yawn.

Hate you, love you, like you, none of those things, I'll say. You're like everyone else in this mall---casual hand gesture---a stranger. I don't know you and don't want to know you. You're a follower. You had nothing but contempt for your family because your friends were like that and you wanted to be accepted by them. Everything you said or did, every lie you told, showed your contempt for us. And when you realized we weren't going to let you use us anymore, you turned your back on us. Who wants to know someone like that?

She'll be ready to defend herself and to bring up every real or imagined slight she suffered during all those years she lived at home. She'll be eager to debate me, to prove that she's the victim. She'll strain forward, up on the balls of her feet, fists clenched. And then she'll deflate when she sees the indifference on my face. She'll turn and walk away, shoulders slumped.

For a while I'll watch the other strangers coming and going through the mall, looking for familiar faces. There will be only one, turning a corner and coming toward me, smiling. I'll smile back when she's close enough to see my face, but I won't tell my wife a thing.

THE LAST RECORD STORE
by Corey Mesler

You walk into the last record store on Earth. It was quite a trek to get there. The clerk has complicated hair and a tattoo that says, "John Lives Here." You say to him, "I need that music from that film. The one where the guy meets the gal and she and he do things that people in movies mostly don't do." The clerk says, "You're talking about Johnny Dark and the Fictioneers." It doesn't sound right but you've come a long way. "Look," you say, "Give me that and the one where the female singer sounds like a train colliding with a tangerine." On the walk home you realize that it wasn't that movie at all. It was the sequel to the one about the dying Stoic, the one with all the midges. Still, Johnny Dark rings a vague bell. He sounds like Quasimodo. He sounds like your mother. In your review you say, "It's the kind of music you'd walk to the ends of the Earth for."

BLACK ONYX
by Clare Needham

Marie is taken by the hand and led down the hall. She walks over carpet, her feet make no sound. The kind woman leading Marie—she guesses the woman is kind from the pleasant feel of the skin, the firm grasp-- keeps her back to her, and has no face. At intervals mounted on the wall are soft yellow lamps, their shades in the shape of tulips that curve over the bulb. Marie recognizes the form, recalls a similar light she had when she was a girl.

When they reach the door the woman disappears. Marie is alone in a bedroom, familiar yet not: the bedspread has a pattern of small blue flowers, and there is her nightstand; one opened closet door shows the drapes of her clothes--but the dimensions of the room are strange. Much grander, the ceiling higher, the walls further from the bed, and it takes time, it takes too much time, to move from the threshold to the foot of the bed, where she stands and sees, to her delight, an elegant set of clothes laid out in the imprint of a human form.

From nowhere come attendants. Ladies, all murmuring in soothing voices, none with an individual face, their voices rising and falling, beckon Marie to undress and try on the clothes they have so carefully prepared.

There is a dress, black, which slides easily over her ready body; the length is long and the sleeves are long. There's a slight dip around the neck and in back; the fabric puffs dramatically at the shoulders, but the dress is made of thick and modest cloth. It feels surprisingly cool.

She sits down. A lady kneels before her, one hand holding Marie's ankle, while the other eases on a pair of high-laced shoes with hook and eye fastenings, reminiscent of figure skates. Her arms are taken and held at length. Cold leather gloves, smooth and supple, are slipped onto each hand. "I won't be needing these," says Marie. "It's too much," she murmurs a minute later. General coo of disagreement--gentle disagreement. The gloves stay on. A jewelry box is brought forth, the lid opened: gold bracelets inlaid with black onyx, and heavy earrings, too heavy for her to wear.

Marie's gloved hand hovers, swoops down and slips on a bracelet. "These are too lovely," she says. She turns her wrist, and the bracelet glows with light caught from an unseen source.

With great love and great care, Marie's hair is pinned up with fancy combs. Marie cannot remember having ever received such treatment. The dress-up game--for this is what it is, with these strange and old-fashioned clothes--comes to an end when Marie is brought to her feet. She is at the door again, and when it opens, she notices that the door is no longer at the end of the hall as it once was: the hall has extended itself further and deeper, and then she is walking, walking again, her hand intertwined with the kind lady's.

They walk quickly. Marie is certain of her body, of the direction in which she is being taken. She is walking, she now realizes, into her grave. There is but one way to go. Down the hall. She half-wants the walk to never end, the kind woman to hold her hand firmly, press down like that forever; she half-wants to be alone, to take this walk by herself. Really alone, forever.

MOVEMENT
by Timothy Norton

The cable was received at 6:03 a.m. on Thursday the 8th. Others were received at 6:04 a.m. and 6:05 a.m. and throughout the day in a hall chattering like hail falling on tin roofs. Men and women paced about, went in and out of the hall, listened to others speaking, made some points, deliberated, discussed, calls coming in passed through like beams of light finding a place to give off heat.

One of the women looked at the cables briefly and moved again to join the mass swarming like bees. One of the men passed and did the same. Someone stopped nearby with a thought on the brain, maybe from a draft or a tightening of the chest, turned toward the cable and snatched it up in hand. That was what it was, what the hail was about, the light after the storm, the honey for the bees. Eyes opened wide, mind escaping the body, glancing around at the others, listening, mute, seeing the hail from the sky. Giving it to the secretary, it was scanned, assimilated into the network, the infrastructure, and one by one as the men and women left to go to their places, they saw the cable of ten sentences in front of them as it painted a picture as certain as time. A pause, deep breath, mind exits and enters body, and then the words flowed like wind rushing up the side of a mountain.

The mountain stood nowhere and was composed of nothing of substance, but it was there as surely as day. Up at the top was a power plant creating a swath of light to brighten the mountain. The light hit a blade of grass, growing its roots and dislodging a rock, which collected at the bottom with some others to bake under the sun. A current of wind absorbed the heat and swept across the bottom to the other side where it was embodied at 7:29 p.m. in a hall with men and women bustling about.

A man with an eye awry lay in repose under the roof of his villa. His legs were spread across his bed with his hand hanging limply off. A bee buzzed around his face as he swatted it away. He shut one eye, then the other, squinted, looked around the room. Through the window glinted a bright reflection he wasn't sure he saw. Startled, he ran to the window. A warm breeze blew off the valley. There it was, the spark, never seen before. It was the way the light careened off the leaves in a color he'd never seen, sprang across the vintner's roof and raced down into the shade of the valley, captured by the gush of wind, rushing and churning. Eyes closed, he saw it and the limp hand went to work a moment later, soaking up light from the scene as it sent its warmth across the valley.

And it happened again, just like before. Next time the woman could anticipate it from these findings. It was all possible because of the new technique she developed to measure the cascade down into the valley. She looked toward the top, took in a breath and felt the warm ground under her hand. This would cause earthquakes, no doubt. She handed the discovery to the businessperson who found a new method to replicate the results she made possible.

One day she rested by a creek and tried to discern what the valley would look like if she had designed it, then a disturbance, an anomaly provoked an ineffable stir in her mind. Frustrated, she knew what happened and could prove it, but how? Years burning in her chest, tension at every fingertip, and it traveled down to her fingers, shaping together a completed puzzle. It would all be taken into account, everything.

Once it was finished, she and the businessperson took the march up the valley, not sure of when they reach the highest point, the place where it came from, but they had the results forever. They found the highest point possible and drew up the plans to build that thing bubbling under their skins, deep in their mind and out the fingertips of labor, making the view from the valley a little better.

Up, down, through and through, again and again, once again, another time, perfectly all the time, always, spin, wrestle, thrust, faster, faster, they worked as an engine on the engine. The drone throughout, the metal and machinery, human made metal, metal made human--and there, resting in the center of the revolutions of the engines powering the engine powering a beam of light as if it were life itself. Then a break from work, engine still turning, a laugh a shove a smile. The breeze outside is strong, but unnoticed until it blows a film of dust across the beam, reflecting part of the source of the beam into the machine altering the beam. That is all. Silence and awe, not a word about it but exclamations, but they feel it and return to the grind of metal. No one looks at the beam; they take commands from their bodies and are machines powering machines—to look at it would blind anyone.

No one has seen this. No one knows if any of this even exists. They believe in it though, because they take orders from their guts. The people in the hall have never been in the machine, the laborers have never been in the villa, the businessperson and scientist have never been in the hall. In all likelihood, none of this is here, but people are able to discuss, labor, observe, inspire and make. And within each person a story is made whole as we set the world in motion.

SHRINE
by Meg Pokrass

He was meticulously rude. Sometimes profoundly nice. When we weren't arguing, we'd snuggle under our effective sweat-box comforter, fraying from so many happy and sad years of sex and sweat and cat dander. The whole world seemed to be tanning or wrinkling.

The police popped in one night to see if we were using drugs or if our fights were murderous.

We'd been arguing loudly in the kitchen about the texture of a birthday cake I'd baked for the birthday of our second dead dog. It was hard as a rock, and nothing had ever been different. Arguing was part of the cake-eating experience.

When I heard the doorbell ring, I snuck from the kitchen into the bedroom.

"Hello, sir, mind if we enter?" a voice said, two voices coughed.

"Do you own any weapons, sir?" I heard the cop ask my husband.

It sounded like there were fifteen people, like horses and villagers or showgirls. Lots of feet. A dog toy squeaked.

"Whoops!" one of them said.

"With a chef like my Prozac-bride? Weaponry with this woman here?" then a scratchy minute of silence, my ear to the door.

"Where did she go?"

The cop's voice said, "What woman, sir. Where?"

"Where did she go?"

One of the cops giggled a girly giggle. The talkative one sniffed the air and said, "Um. Interesting scent."

He was referring to the stench of marijuana we'd used up, or else the rat cage. It was time for me, so I idled into the living room wearing my "Munch Me" shortie nightshirt, and my long-nosed barracuda slippers. Not much else. My legs were still shapely, and tan from bronzing gel.

"Hey! I recognize you! I know your mom!" I said to the young cop. He was adorable, with dirty blond hair and an ape-like neck.

He smiled sheepishly and said, "We didn't mean to disturb your evening, ma'am."

Clicking over to him with my vixen slippers, I looked him over the way Lauren Bacall looked at Bogart in the Big Sleep and said, "You know how to whistle?"

"Ha," my husband said. "Who would kill her? Would you kill her?"

After they left, my husband grabbed one of the packaged condoms from our shrine. It was pretty tall, at least forty piled, wrapped sheep skin condoms, and three diaphragms of slightly different sizes looking like alien hats. It had the shape of a welt of sadness, sat in the corner of our bedroom surrounded by a crowd of dust-bunnies.

I was too old to get pregnant--and he was too old to do much, but I was glad to live alone with him in the kingdom of mammals. Sometimes, I really was.

SUMMER GUN
by Meg Pokrass

Mother was not insidious, the way my sister said, but she did hide a lot of things in her briefcase. Things that clinked. People never liked that she excelled at being unaccountable, and that she treated us as if we were her fan club, not her kids.

It was easy to see why there was little magic between her and other females.

Mother said often that she was stupid enough to marry once, and botch most of everything...but she was not stupid enough to keep digging a hole once she was in it.

Father left when Mother started keeping a summer gun in a fashion holster around her skirt. After he left, he sent us many postcards, none of which said anything about returning.

He would write things like: "Dears, I am writing to you both from my brand new thrift-store desk!"

And, "You remember that enormous wrinkle on my forehead? It has vanished!"

"Girls, my lips are much less chapped!"

The very last one he sent, and then they stopped forever, said, "There is virtue in being a little wishful."

We sometimes wondered if we would have been better off with no parents at all, living in an orphanage, with the sympathy of bosomy women whispering about how cute we were.

My sister would shush me when mother talked about her long business trip to Spain, and that we were so ready to take care of ourselves, and how much fun we would all have on separate continents.

I wanted to say, "Legally, I think you are burning a Motherhood contract" but my sister said once mother was gone, we could drown our problems with good holiday cheer, and I knew what she meant. We knew where the good stuff was stashed, and the feeling grew in stature and possibility... the idea of mother so far away and us so in charge of the five animals, finding them holiday costumes (the dogs) and making our own holiday cards and getting good at light cooking and using the corner market and maybe finding some very funny movies. And backrubs were easy enough, we gave them to each other when times were tough.

We could always call our father, when and if we found his new phone number, we would feel much more like children. In the meantime, we'd give each other "real dad" advice, and because we'd make it up, the world was full of cheer.

THE LONESOME ALIEN
by Robert Pope

I wake up from this dream where ALIENS
HAVE LANDED in little round saucers like you
always imagined, pouring out looking like clichés. One
in a beret and beard, black turtleneck, a copy of *Nausea*
under one arm—beatnik, no less—half a dozen
cowboys, a couple Chicago gangsters from the forties.
Pinup girls and Eleanor Roosevelt arm in arm like
they've been watching TV on planet Couch Potato!

So I get up, pull on my favorite duds and join the
freak show. The jeans are beauties, tight and pegged,
white socks and pointy-toe boots. All I need in these
duds is a white t-shirt, black leather jacket. A little
Brylcreem in my hair, comb it in a curl in front, duck
ass in the back. I'm ready to rock, tips of my fingers in
my pockets, way too tight for anything else. I'm in the
swing, bopping around town, coming up to people
saying, "Greetings, Earthling! Take me to your leader.
I come in peace."

I'm doing this a couple hours, and it starts to wear
on me. No one digs what I'm up to so I go looking
for a pool hall. I get in this big fight and have to kick a
little ass, not to mention getting my ass kicked a little.

Knives are definitely drawn. I'm backed against a dirty brick wall in an alley, spotlight from somewhere, and I'm saying, "Hey, man, you gotta dig me! Take me to your leader."

But they keep coming on, and I'm explaining, "I come in peace!" These guys start looking at each other like, "Is this guy nuts?" I'm saying, "Dig me, man, I'm an alien—from another friggin planet!" I point at the sky and a couple of these guys look behind, so I take the chance to run right through them. They're on my heels, and I'm not saying anything, just running like hell! I cut through a mall, yelling, "Out of my way! Alien haters on my trail!"

Once I lose them down a side street I stop in a diner for a burger, but I'm shaking, can't eat, so I order up a cup of coffee. My hand is jiggling bad. I'm spilling coffee on the counter, trying to tell the counterman what's up. "I'm an alien, man. I got freaking antennae in my hair. Cut me a little slack!"

He leans over the counter, tells me to bug off *pronto*. Long story short, I'm back to my pad late, all shook up. I fall in the sack, stare up at the ceiling. Earthlings can be so cold! I pass out and here comes the dream again, only this time we're heading back to the saucers, looking over our shoulders, and I'm running with an *actual* Martian—totally green and naked with bug eyes and retractable antennae!

Me and this Martian climb in a saucer, slam up the juice and split, speaking with some extra sensory reception. He's saying, "We must find a planet open to immigration." I'm saying, "You said a mouthful." In a minute we're light years through the galaxy, and I'm wondering if there's anyone on earth who'll look

for Skeezix in the morning. Anyone who'll miss the
hell out of me?

SHAPE SHIFTER
by Robert Pope

Old Mrs. Timber came up behind them when she saw all three cats hissing at the rain-streaked window from the back of the couch. She had seen the gold dog a little earlier, running around her back yard, but she had never seen the muddy brown one.

Her first impulse was to call someone—but whom? Did they have dog catchers in white vans with cages in back? The men would wear white coats, carry nets on poles, or poles electrified, those things police use to shock a man off his feet.

Something should be done about the dogs, but all she wanted was to get them out of her annuals and forget them. She could go outside and shoo them, but what if they were mean or rabid?

If she went out she should have protection, perhaps a poker from the fireplace. She glanced to make certain they were there. Hal had loved a fire. She liked it too, but since he passed there had been no fires.

Those dogs could make a mess of flowerbeds, but they seemed to be having fun. She hated to threaten, but decided on the largest butcher knife in the holder on the kitchen counter. She held it like buttering toast, but if one decided to attack she could give it a good poke. She should really find her glasses, but there wasn't time.

She went to the door and called, "You dogs! Stop that! Stop that now."

They looked at her, all covered in mud. It was inexcusable, the way people let dogs out without leash or collar. Hodges rubbed against her, watching the dogs around her legs—too much for the dogs. They ran at her, first the gold, then the muddy brown. Hodges took off around the house, the dogs on his tail.

"Hodges," she wailed. Tears rolled down her cheeks. Hodges had been her first cat after Hal had passed. She loved the glossy black of him, the aqua eyes. "Hodges!"

The other two cats stood on the porch, looking around the side of the house where Hodges disappeared. "Shoo," she cried, waving the knife at them. "Get back where you belong." They allowed her to corral them through the door and shut it after before she went around the house.

She set a hand against the bricks as she stood at the back corner. They were coming at her, the terrified Hodges in the lead. The cat ran past on her left, dogs on the right, tangling in her dress for the briefest moment, enough that her feet went sliding forward and she slid on her back.

"Oh! Oh!" she cried, brandishing the knife, waving it about. She managed to roll on her stomach and lift her body on her arms, cautious of the dogs.

With her fingers wrapped around the handle of the knife, she crawled until she stood and made her way back to the front door.

Once there she could not open the door, as it locked automatically when she shut it after Tetty and Queen Anne, watching from the window. She heard wild barking in the distance and sat on the porch weeping.

Then Hodges slinked along the house front toward her, wet and disheveled as she had ever seen him, with such bright eyes. "Hodges! Oh, thank God—those horrible dogs!"

She held out her arms and noticed the butcher knife in her right hand. Hodges screeched and leaped onto her head. Mrs. Timber screamed and sliced the air blindly as they rushed on her again. "You beasts!" she cried. She stabbed the air—the blade slid into something soft and stopped.

When she opened her eyes, Hodges was nowhere to be seen, but, lying near, head and shoulders cocked up on the porch, was a muddy little boy, handle of the butcher knife protruding from his throat, darkness spreading from the point of entry.

She covered her mouth with both hands. At one moment she saw a brown dog, at another, a little boy she could not recognize for the mud. She tried to stand and stumbled onto him. She took hold of the knife, extracting it from his throat—dark liquid spreading thicker on his shirt.

She stood at last and broke the glass of the small window on her door with the handle, and then reached through and turned the latch. She looked about as she went to her knees and clutched the boy under his arms.

She heard the crash of thunder as the rain came harder. She tugged until the body budged. Her terror gave her strength to drag the boy inside and close the door.

On the hardwood floor of her foyer lay the little boy. She closed her eyes, opened them, but he was still there. She clutched him beneath the arms, but gave up. She stood and took his ankles in her hands and dragged him toward the kitchen. He moved more easily across the floor.

She leaned against the wall to breathe and set in once more, trailing three black cats, all speaking at the same time. She dropped his feet, opened the basement door, and pushed his shoulders through. At last she heard him tumble down the stairs. She turned the key and hid it in the flour canister.

She did not stop until she cleaned the floor and blocked the broken window with cardboard from an old shoebox. She pulled the curtains closed and sat before the television, her cats around her, Hodges in her lap. An old black-and-white flickered from the screen, but that is not what she was watching—not at all.

YOU AND PJ
AND MOLLY AND ZACK
by Susan Powers

Okay, say you don't remember the day PJ flipped. Even thinking about that day, what would you say? The police arrived, they handcuffed him and drove him to the mental ward of some hospital? You might say that, but that would not be quite true. To reveal the truth would be to violate the silent pact between you. And much happened before the police arrived, and so much more before that. So much you can not speak of, think about. Ever.

According to PJ, that is the problem: you. You have some big problem about which he won't say specifically, but apparently *you* are also the source of all the problems between you. Of course this is PJ talking, having flipped out. You try to remember this when he claims that, in fact, it is your alleged silence about your supposed problems that is making him sick. You catch the word 'sick' and hang onto it, grateful that it belongs to him. You stand in the bedroom preparing to go to work, to drive to the suburbs, to earn the money that helps you both to live how you live.

Nicely, you thought. Then he blocks you from leaving and screams in your face, "*You're sick – you!*"

And you think for a moment, maybe it's true. True enough that you start to shake.

You flee to the bathroom and call Molly and Zack from your cell phone. Days earlier you'd revealed some particulars of the situation to them. You were not relieved to admit these, but knew that you might need their help. Now you call, asking.

Then there's banging on the bathroom door, and PJ talking in tongues: Russian, Spanish Pomeranian (you guess).

Months seem to pass, and then Molly and Zack arrive. You are almost surprised when PJ allows them to enter. But he's wanted witnesses. Now he has witnesses, and one of them, Molly, the outspoken one among you, says, "PJ, we'll take you to the hospital. You need to go. You need to come with us."

PJ grabs the phone to call the police. *We* are out of control, he yells in quick Spanish. Like a bolt of lightning, he is first at one end of the house and then the other. Zack lets out an involuntary laugh. Molly's face folds. You think of a cartoon.

Of course you don't watch cartoons. You are a professor of Economics, a woman who prefers concrete numbers and the intrigue of analysis to silliness and improbable fantasy. You have chosen this profession because it is aligned with your principles and with what you know how best to do. So you think about the idea of a cartoon, a generic cartoon. The idea, of course, does not amuse you. You remember a different PJ, funny, smart, agreeable. Who is this PJ, you wonder, and understand right then there will be

no discussion of this day (if this day should ever pass)
or of any other day for that matter, and certainly not of
the days that led up to this one. Though in truth, as
you listen to PJ calling the police on you and your
friends, you can not think of how this all began.

Was it the day PJ came home and claimed his
grandfather had spoken to him from the grave? Yes,
he said "grave," certain of the location of the ethereal
voice. That day you checked his eyes for evidence of
drugs and found no evidence.

Or maybe it was the first night he didn't sleep,
and for many weeks afterwards could be found
walking, running, pacing the house all night, singing
his favorite show tunes and holding conversations with
some specter. You began to sleep in separate rooms,
locking your door at night. You needed your rest, you
said.

Or it might have begun with the 'things' that
started to appear in the house, first piled in corners,
then filling the spare room, then spilling throughout all
the rooms. Or when he started hiding the things he
bought in his car until he could no longer safely drive
the car and you discovered evidence that your bank
account was overdrawn and savings were being
charged fees, due to lack of funds. These were the
signs, but until his co-workers emailed you telling you
he'd barked—literally—at the boss and was sent home
to "rest," you did not dare think what this could mean,
or how to get help.

Now he's called the police, and here they are.
Soon there is shouting, scuffling, loud commanding
voices, and you hide in the bedroom, your heart
shuddering. When he at last agrees to check himself

into a hospital, it is Molly and Zack who drive him there.

The hospital stay levels him out. He takes meds, and grows silent and unnervingly somber, but so unlike the hyper, babbling PJ of the last couple of months, you breathe a sigh of relief. And slowly, methodically, he starts to unclutter his car, the house, his life. You get to stay, the unspoken agreement between you that nothing of what happened would be discussed by you or him, or by you and Molly, or by you and Zack, (though it might be discussed between Molly and Zack), but between you and PJ and Molly and Zack, it would all just disappear into the past, into a cavern of silence, while your life begins anew, so quiet and calm, that some, even you, mistake it for peace.

LIKE NOURISHMENT
by Susan Powers

In the camps, while all around her the starving died, says the landlady, the less she ate, the better she felt. As if nothingness were something, as if hollowness were not the same thing as emptiness, she grew. She grew breasts, developed hips, developed muscles firm and round in her arms and legs. Her dusty brown eyes sparkled, her thinning hair gleamed; still, she did not eat. Those strong enough to lift their heads regarded her passively. Guards took notice, things happened to her. Things she doesn't talk about. Things she's kept inside of her, filling her like nourishment.

WHEN IT BURST
by Joshua Rigsby

It was the shovel that did him in. The blockage near his heart had strained for too many years to keep up with drive-thrus and late-night binges. On occasion the man wondered if he noticed a palpitation or shortness of breath, but never imagined that something was lurking in his chest plotting his demise. It always let just enough blood slip by to keep from being noticed, but now the pressure had reached critical mass. The artery was as sealed as the poor man's fate. It was as the shovel struck the ground at the end of a satisfying day's work that it happened. He was not prepared.

The day before, Dr. Stephen Maud drove into his driveway a defeated man. The sun had just set beyond the poplars across the street. He sighed and let his head sink forward until it touched the steering wheel. After slowly gathering his resolve, he forced himself to step out of the car, walk to the front door, and enter his one-story brick home.

Stephen Maud was a Linguistics professor at a nearby university. He was in his late forties, medium height, with a balding head and a penchant for tweed suit coats. His life revolved around words. The walls of his home were covered with books about words. Etymologies, lexicons, dictionaries, thesauruses, he lived off of the form, substance and meaning of words.

He flicked on the yellow light of his study room and collapsed into his armchair with a sigh. His fingers felt their way over his furrowed brow trying to massage away his sense of frustration and inability to comprehend his situation. He stayed awake throughout the night alternately pacing the length of his study and going back to the kitchen to pour another cup of Earle Grey. His mind pondered his condition until he had reduced it all, sum and substance down to one word. He jostled the word around in his brain. He chewed on it. He spat it out and dissected it. His inner-discussions sometimes became quite lively and he would raise his voice and exclaim with catharsis the ideas that were coursing through his stream of consciousness. Other times, though, he would sit, quiet and sullen afraid to touch the word as though it were a rapacious, man-eating beast staring at him from across the room.

Full of fears and contradictions Dr. Maud fought with himself throughout the night until the deep blue of dawn began to give forms to the dark figures of trees and buildings outside his window. He heard his alarm go off in the bedroom. Time to move forward. He left his study and proceeded with his morning as he normally would. He ate breakfast, showered, dressed, and went to work.

He met his good friend Michael Donavan over lunch. The two had gotten close as Dr. Maud walked him through his dissertation. He was a good student, now an adjunct faculty member, young, vivacious, handsome, optimistic. Dr. Maud asked him to come to his house for dinner.

The two of them strolled through his backyard that evening.

"Michael, I've asked you here because I would like to talk with you about something."

"What would that be?" the young professor asked.

"Irony."

Michael looked up wondering if it was a trick or a trap. The professor was always playing with the words he used, any time he spoke he placed them upside down in awkward syntaxes just to get a rise out of the unprepared.

Dr. Maud looked away from his protégé and responded distantly. "Because I am out of time. I have six months to a year. Cancer. Brain cancer, of all things. Can you believe that? I speak six different languages. I've written thirty books and mountains of articles. I spent my whole life reading, memorizing facts, and developing my mind. All for nothing. My brain is going to pull the trigger in the end… Irony."

"Six months to a year?" Michael responded.

"This monks do ya hear?" Dr. Maud punned uncontrollably. "I've often wondered what 'monking' might entail… I usually gave up wondering when I consider the copious silence it would no doubt involve."

"Well, at least you have some time left… right? Who knows…" Michael's voice trailed off. Both men stood silent. Michael rejoined the attack on his friend's morbid revelation. "What sort of work do you need done around here? I have the rest of the evening free. I enjoy working when the mind is vexed."

Dr. Maud tilted his head to one side as he considered it. "I bought a sapling yesterday, but I didn't have the heart to put it in the ground. It was hard to think of anything else. You know?"

"Certainly."

Dr. Maud pulled the shovel from a pile of gardening utensils and pointed to the spot where he wanted the tree to go.

"Let me dig first until I get tired." The professor said.

Michael watched quietly from his grassy backyard seat as Dr. Maud plunged the shovel into the dark, warm earth. They talked about normal things: baseball, politics, what their plans entailed when the semester was finished. Michael cheered himself with the idea that he had calmed the old professor down and helped him to see things in a rational light once again. A little physical exercise will do that for you.

Michael stood and extended his hand, "Here, let me try for a while, you look a little winded. We shouldn't go too much deeper or the sapling won't be able to breathe." He jabbed the shovel into the dirt, and heaved out the last spade-full of soil.

That was when it burst.

KARLISKI WALKS
by JL Schneider

He sees a bee figure eight in front of him, then buzz up the long driveway toward the road. He follows it.

He shuffles onto county highway 421, the shiv of his slippers on the macadam accompanied by the syncopated click of his cane. Baby steps. Globes of lilacs over his head. Sniffing up and smelling—*Where's my wife?* He's alone on the road, shuffling past the houses, untrimmed forsythia, and lily jungles in the ditches. The mountain air. *I have friends somewhere on this road.*

He urinates in his pants.

Baby steps. Up a hill. Baby steps. A car swerves around him at the last minute, horn blaring. *I have to get there.* He giggles. He has a dream.

The other wife, from long ago. His hands are young and strong. He watches them swing open-palmed through the air, steel swatters smacking front and back across her face. He closes them into fists.

They're like iron balls at the ends of his wrists, crushing a bone in her face. Her young pretty face. Her tender flawless skin mottling before his eyes. He looks down at his thin, brittle wrists, the emerging corpse we will become.

Lilacs by the road, French whites, the same fat silky clusters he pushed his face into as if they were breasts.

Down the hill, baby steps.

That house. That house. Not that house in the wind. Wild pink dogwood petals swirl around him, pelting his face, one soft rouge kiss sticking to the spittle on his chin.

The years—cabbage and potatoes, his favorite meal. Friday nights. Saturday nights. His wild fists swinging at the air.

Baby steps, faster. *Where is my wife?* He's chewing on the air, falling. He's on his hands and knees in the middle of the road, licking gravel off his lips. A car comes over the hill. He hears it behind him. He turns and watches the hubcaps spin past, reaching out to touch them, as if reaching for doughnuts, the air.

Where are my friends?

Dot and Lily, his neighbors coming home after their shifts at the Luncheonette and the prison, find him in the middle of the road. They pick him up. Each grabs an arm, finally meeting him. They look at each other across the back of his neck, as if they can still hear the first wife screaming. From different sides of the road, in those days…They were only wives.

Where's my dog?

He turns his head and blows hard through his nose. A ball of snot jets down and lands on top of

Dot's stockinged foot. Another car rushes past. He giggles.

"Where do you want to go, Mr. Karliski?" Dot asks him.

I have friends in that house. He points to Dot's house.

"No. That's my house. Do you want to go home? We'll take you home. Where's your wife?"

He looks up and searches the sky. The smell of fresh urine fills the air.

The women turn him around and start him back up the hill. Baby steps. The *shiv shiv shiv* of his slippers. Lily's hissing through her teeth when she steps on a pebble. Dot's arthritis. He's smiling between the women. He's a little boy, pure white breasts pressed against his cheeks, his little nose buried in the cleft and his brain liquored with peace and beauty.

"If we let him go, someone will eventually hit him," Lily whispers. She steps on a stone—hiss. Dot stops the three of them, looks up and down the empty road, then pulls them forward again.

They walk down the long driveway to his house and sit him down. The sun fills the bench in front of his house. Dot wipes her palms hard on her apron. He looks up at them. He starts sobbing, then abruptly stops. When they leave, he gets up and follows them.

The women guide him back to the bench, then sit down on either side of him. Each of them takes one of his hands and holds it. He is beaming between them. They wait. They wait all afternoon for the second wife to come home. They've seen her out on warm days, smiling, walking slowly up and down the roads.

SEASIDE HITCHHIKER
by Bob Thurber

The moon was full and bright. Its yellow glow had followed me like a searchlight across thirty miles of interstate. On the curling beach road I slowed as I took the bend, admiring the wavering line the moon spread on the ocean, when a girl swept across my high beams, her thumb high. I merely tapped the brakes, but the road was sandy and the rear of the car hooked. I skidded then spun to a stop like some high school punk showing off for his prom date.

She opened the passenger door and leaned in. A white long-sleeved shirt, soaking wet, clung to her swimsuit like lace. The car's dome shone in her eyes. She was somewhere between sixteen and twenty.

"Thanks for stopping, mister."

"I can't take you far, just up the road a bit.

She gave a polite grin, shrugged. "Every little bit helps," and slid onto the seat.

Her hair hung like tangled seaweed and she stunk

of the ocean, but she was attractive enough.

Once we got going, she twisted the rear-view mirror and lined her lips with a tube of pink lipstick. I kept one eye on the road, which ran parallel with the shoreline.

"There's a mirror above the visor," I said.

She puckered and dabbed. "This one's fine."

After she finished she tucked the lipstick into her shirt pocket. It bulged there, like a bullet. I readjusted the mirror. She caught me looking, moved her tongue across her teeth.

"You always swim at night," I said.

"Not always."

"You live around here?"

"Close enough."

"Year round, or just for the summer?"

She pushed a hand through her hair. "I shouldn't be telling you this, but I'm actually a mermaid, so I kind of live everywhere around here."

"A mermaid, huh?"

"That's right."

My turn was just ahead. "Where'd you get the lipstick? At the mermaid mall?"

"Found it. In the sand."

I tilted my head to see her legs. "Where are your fins?"

"Don't be silly. That's just myth."

I laughed, a little choking cough. She was either crazy or stoned. I held the wheel steady and sped past my turn. Our clapboard cottage, a summer rental my wife had found, was visible from this distance but I didn't look to see if lights were on.

"Your parents know you're out this late?"

"It's not late."

"It's after midnight."

She shrugged. "My parents are dead. Sharks ate them."

"Sharks, huh?"

She shuddered. "Sharks gobble up mermaids the way you people eat potato chips."

I thought about letting her off, turning back. My wife was on vacation, but I wasn't. I had another long commute in the morning. "How do you know what people eat?"

"Oh, I come ashore a lot. To visit. I'm not afraid of people, just sharks."

"Where do you sleep?"

"Depends."

"You sleep on the beach?"

"Sometimes. But I really hate the smell of rotting seaweed. I much prefer a bed."

"A little sea bed?"

"That's funny." She brought one knee up onto the seat. It bumped my thigh. "Have any money?"

"Why," I said.

She waited a while before answering. "There are motels up on the main strip. About five miles."

I knew about those motels. Ramshackle places. My wife had looked into their weekly rates, calculated the cost against the beach house.

"You hungry?" I said.

She shook her head.

"I'm hungry," I said.

She stuck her face out the window. The back of her blouse puffed and fluttered.

"So what do you do for money? How do you pay

for food, motels?"

She twisted into a kneeling position, got her entire head and shoulders outside the car. Her swimsuit cut high on her thighs.

"Oh, I never pay," she said.

The Brine Motel was a line of small cabins beside an empty swimming pool. I paid in cash and took the key. The room was a box. It stunk of disinfectant.

I asked if she preferred the light on or off and she laughed. "Makes no difference to me."

I like to see what I'm doing, so I left the bathroom's light on. Its glow spread a halo into the room. She undressed beneath the covers, peeling off one wet thing after another. I piled my clothes on a chair. She threw back the blanket, smiled as I climbed onto her.

"What's your name," I said.

"You'd never be able to pronounce it."

She kissed me on the mouth, then wiggled her hips, working her body down to get me centered. She held my ass with one hand and guided my penis with the other.

"At least tell me how old you are."

She shushed me, kissed my neck. "Honey, relax. By human standards, I'm a hundred years past legal."

She was slippery and tight, and she knew how to work her groin muscles. I didn't last five minutes.

"Jesus," I said, pulling breath. I hadn't gotten my wind when she nudged me off her. I rolled and flopped. I looked at the ceiling, then closed my eyes. Lying there felt familiar and I decided this was my wife's fault. Somehow she was to blame.

I started to drift, then jerked awake, certain the

girl had swiped my wallet, taken my car.

But she was right there, huddled on the edge of the bed. I could only see half her face, but she appeared older now, with hard creases along the side of her mouth.

She stretched her arms into a yawn. "I hate to be a prude, but I need to get some sleep." She threw her head back in an exaggerated fashion.

"I'm still hungry," I said, and reached for her.

I pulled her down and tried to pin her but she twisted free. She scrambled to her feet, backed away.

"Hey, look. You're a nice guy and all, but paying for a room doesn't make me your property. I think you better leave now."

But then I showed her my shark teeth.

RELINQUISHING UNDERWATER PARALLAX DELIRIUM
by M. Kaat Toy

Our shell-shocked hero patiently observed the
worst mountebank roofers led by a Cyclops remove
the shingles on their rented, two-bedroom duplex, the
one his wife, a dislocated military brat like they both
were, wouldn't move out of for twenty years through
the births and growing of their daughter and son and
her endless knitting of a shroud. After a storm
seemingly sent by Poseidon tore the exposed tarpaper
off, the wandering family, squabbling like sailors,
searched for a house. His wife rejected each one;
they all failed to suit her for mostly good reasons,
he recalled after she finally found a favorite and
they brought the cat. It died, not unexpectedly,
while she subjected our hero to the test of the bed.
How did it become rooted in the living room? he
wondered silently. At work, his colleague, the lotus
eater, committed suicide. No one knew what to say.
Then the one person who had mentioned he had a

nice voice suffered a brain aneurysm while mimicking
impassioned speeches to the gods. While his
steadfast Penelope remained reluctant to order her
household, our hero burbled how to tread water until
his men, their ears stopped, drowned. Hearing his
requiem sung by Sirens, he struggled to unlash himself.
While his wife's eyes rolled back in a seizure from
his disturbing activities, he shot to the surface of the
dream he had created.

SUMMPLEMENTAL OXYGEN
by Eric Scott Tryon

Simon was traveling a great distance. From Chile.
The thin strip of rock and desert that keeps South
America from sliding into the Pacific. Two years ago
he was sent to San Pedro de Atacama. NASA was
sending a new instrument into the troposphere.

Rita never knew how to respond when he wrote
about science. But she waited anxiously for emailed
pictures of giant salt flats, sleeping volcanoes, and rock
formations that made her own Utah desert look like a
sandbox. When she got word that he planned to
abandon his tented home at the end of the earth to
come meet her for the first time, her heart beat in her
ears. She cleaned the baseboards and swung a broom
at cobwebs that hung from the ceiling.

When the plane took off from Santiago, Simon
felt as if he were flying downwards instead of up.
Months spent at 17,000 feet, with supplemental
oxygen and dehydrated meatloaf, had left his world up

side down. He pulled his seat upright, picked at the sand under his nails, and wondered what the past two years had done to his skin.

Before leaving for the airport, Rita scrolled through countless emails, reminding herself of how he wrote to her. She prepped the guestroom. Maybe tone was misunderstood. Getting lost somewhere in the entangled email lines that wrapped halfway around the world between their computers.

When the plane's wheels hit the runway, Simon's vision blurred to white, and his head lost all pressure. He placed his ears between his knees and waited for his head to re-tether to his body. Anything he once knew of girls was long ago replaced by spectrometers and the Doppler shift.

As Rita stood along the outer border of baggage claim watching a pregnant woman study the escalators, she considered walking back out the automated doors. Retreating to the safety of well-known scenery.

Simon spotted Rita instantly. She was a glowing version of the girl on his computer. They hugged, but the space between their bodies could have housed mountains.

Seatbelts were fastened and Rita clicked on the radio. There was a commercial about a sofa sale.

"You know," Simon said, "All that rock and desert. It's actually hard, sharp quartz. Chile is all quartz."

"Oh?"

"But no one knows. It's all covered in mud."

"I see."

"Mud that's been hardening and building for centuries. It's like a shell that covers the entire country."

"So how do you know the quartz is really there?"

The commercial ended and a song began.

"Every once in a while. If you're looking for it. You can find patches of beautiful crystalline quartz poking through the mud."

Rita said nothing but tapped at the steering wheel, trying to keep the beat, and they rode on, both staring out the windshield at an unfamiliar landscape.

MY SISTER PAULA
by Eric Scott Tryon

My little sister turned into a block of ice the day Mom left.

"A la chingada!" Dad spat over his shoulder as Mom fired up the station wagon. He only spoke Spanish when he was angry. "Desaparece de mi vida."

It was winter, and normally I hated the cold, the way it always made my neck tense. But because of my sister, I was glad for it. She was the size of a shoebox and probably wouldn't melt for days. But I still couldn't leave her on the living room floor like that, cracker crumbs and wiry carpet threads sticking to her sides.

I cleaned out the freezer. Threw away fish sticks, peas, and strawberry ice cream that no one ever ate. And as I gently placed her in, I whispered, "It'll be okay," not knowing if she could hear me.

I checked the freezer ten times a day to make sure Dad didn't take an ice pick to her, murdering his own daughter to keep his Charanda cold. Each time I opened the door I prayed she had returned to her snot-nosed, pig-tailed self, folded and stuffed in the freezer, fingertips blue, teeth chattering. But each time, there she was, clear and cold with sharp corners.

"En la casa de su amiga," is what Dad said when I asked where Paula was. Just to see what he'd say. Spring and summer had come and gone, and he hadn't spoken to me in English since Mom left.

So I waited until late on a damp Friday night and carefully placed my sister in the red cooler Dad used to fill with beer when we went to the beach. She fit perfectly.

With the cooler in one hand, I rode my bike to the park behind the church. As I climbed the large sloping hill, my thighs burned and my breath appeared before me. Once out of the cooler, I placed my sister at the edge of the hill and gingerly sat down upon her.

And with one shove we were off! My sister and I swooshing down the fresh-cut grass at top speed. The wind chilled my nose and howled in my ears as we flew by giant pine trees. And I swore I heard my sister scream, and I screamed with her, my feet held high, arms outstretched. When we reached the bottom, I tumbled end over end, and we both lay covered in wet grass, laughing and laughing and laughing.

When the pain in my side matched the sting of my cheeks, I held her with two hands and climbed back to the top. We rode the hill two, maybe three dozen times, whooping and hollering together as my toes and fingers went numb.

And then she was gone.

She had melted on the back of my jeans, she had

become drops of water on blades of grass, and she had evaporated into fog-bursts of laughter in the brisk night air.

BEING LINDA MARTEN
by Katy Whittingham

I wasn't always her. I used to me, and I had a cat
named Bobby Mac and a job working for the post
office, but I wasn't a carrier because of my bad knees.

I fed Bobby at 6:00 and then at 5:30 when I got
home from my job for the United States Postal
Service. First the phone messages started asking for
Linda, and I noticed there were always two blackbirds
sitting on the wire outside my window. A friend told
me birds use wire for their nests sometimes and really
mess up your connection, but these birds were just
sitting, always sitting. No, I said to the phone voices
then. No, I said, I was not Linda Marten, until finally
they convinced me.

Bobby was old, but not so old for a cat. If he were
a dog he might have been long dead, but he was always
old, old since he started coming around. He was a
stray, and I adopted him because I always loved cats. I
loved that cat. Linda, they told me, was allergic.

Over the winter, my face slowly changed and the birds finally flew away. The mail began to come with her name on it, and I went into to work to report the problem, but they told me that a Linda Marten did not even work for them; they said I did not work for them. They didn't recognize me; I didn't recognize me. There was a time I didn't leave the house or talk to anyone aside from Bobby because when you don't know who you are, conversation becomes quite difficult. A simple errand like going for groceries became almost impossible and was pointless because I no longer liked my favorite foods.

It wasn't until I woke up at 6:00 to feed Bobby on the coldest day I can remember that I ventured back into the world. My punctual cat was not at the door waiting. He was missing. The only part of my heart that was still mine broke in two. I called the police, but the responding officer seemed less than concerned. "Hey, what's the difference between a cat and a dog?" the officer joked, "dogs come when they're called; cats take a message and get back to you later." His inappropriate brevity did not ease my fears, and I told him, frankly, that I didn't know about dogs, but Bobby never missed breakfast. Bobby did not ignore my calls.

Without offering to come by and help, he suggested I check with the neighbors, but no one wanted to open their door to me. Their faces were familiar, but mine was strange and dirty. My reflection in the glass was strange and dirty. I went home to wash my face and try to cover up my Linda mask when I noticed that I had a phone message. Excitedly, I pressed the button hoping it was news about dear

Bobby. "Linda," the message began, "you need to stop coming to look for my cat, you witch. My daughter is crying right now, afraid you will take Putty away again. Do you like making little girls cry, Linda?"

No, it seemed Linda did not, and with that, the transition was complete. I gave up. What choice did I have? When you have a cat named Bobby Mac and a job at the United States Postal Service, and then you don't, well, you might as well accept yourself as Linda Marten.

THE INFORMANT
by Susan Zurenda

It was one of those things that happened spur of the moment on a Saturday when Tommy saw Cole outside moving the sprinkler across our front yard. After so many years of living next door to one another, we were neither close friends nor mere acquaintances. We were sometime friends. The sometime usually occurring as it had this day when our neighbors invited us to dinner.

I, Libby, insisted on making dessert. And walking across the adjoining driveways with the chocolate torte in one hand, I put my other hand through the crook of Cole's elbow. The gesture made everything seem normal. We looked like any middle-aged couple whose last child had recently left for college and were contented now with only each other.

The evening would be pleasant and predictable. We would drink a lot of wine, listen to music, and hear all the gossip from the highfalutin local society Malinda and Tommy worked hard to keep up with. It had been that way since we became neighbors 16 years before.

I hoped Cole would unwind. I was worried about the long hours he was working. If I said anything, he reminded me he didn't have the luxury of fixed hours at the library like his wife. And if he *was* at home in the early evening, and I tried to connect us in conversation, he would soon lean back in his recliner and say we both needed some downtime.

By the end of the second bottle of wine—our neighbors had mailed home several cases during their recent trip to California wine country—I had begun to feel a soft fuzziness in my head. It was delightful. And Cole was beginning to relax. I watched him tilt his glass straight up to drain purple drops that dribbled across his handsome squared jaw instead of into his mouth and laughed. He stuck out his tongue at me, and it seemed funny so that everyone laughed. It made me think maybe later tonight we would make love.

When Malinda finally set down her glass and went to the kitchen, I rose to help. There was chicken, saffron rice, salad, and the surprise of homemade bread. I presumed the bread had been a gift. The joy of entertaining, not cooking, was Malinda's talent.

I could hear Tommy and Cole discussing wine as they walked toward the dining room. "You'll like this one, buddy," Tommy said. I heard him mention "hint of cinnamon" as Malinda and I arrived bearing dishes into the dining room.

Tommy walked around the table pouring the wine. He leaned over me a little too far so that his hand grasped my shoulder to catch his balance. "Tell me if you like it," he said, straightening up and giving my shoulder another squeeze.

"I'm not a connoisseur," I replied as I lifted the rim of the glass to my lips. "But I know it will taste good." I looked up and Tommy winked. His hand came back to my shoulder again."

"Tommy is flirting with me," I announced and giggled.

Tommy shrugged his shoulders playfully in return. "What can I say? I'm a lucky man in the presence of a woman almost as lovely as my wife." He moved to pour Malinda's wine, and as he did, he kissed her on the cheek. She looked up adoringly. I looked toward Cole, but he was cutting chicken.

Toward the end of the meal, an old R&B song I'd loved as a teenager blasted from the kitchen speakers in a quick explosion. "I Got the Fever," Billy Scott shouted. All of a sudden I was back dancing on a sawdust floor at Myrtle Beach. I jumped up and spun on my heels. My hair slung across my cheek. I felt young.

"Hey, Cole. You might get lucky tonight," Tommy said. His comment was an old joke the men had said to one another forever. "When's the last time Libby danced like this?"

"Dance with me Cole," I said, spinning toward him.

"You seem to be doing fine on your own," he said.

"Very well, then. While I'm up, I'll dance my way to the bathroom."

"Tell me what you think," Malinda called. "I've redecorated."

I switched on the light, and a chandelier with

crystal teardrops dazzled above my head. The walls were deep green, nearly black. I looked into the gilded frame of a too-large mirror as I descended onto the toilet. "Whoa," I said aloud. "Mighty flashy."

The knob of the bathroom door turned, and I started up, alarmed. I was afraid Malinda had overheard me. I stood to pull up my pants, worrying about how to remedy my remark.

But it was Tommy. "Sshhh," he whispered. He came inside and shut the door.

"What are you doing?" I said. "I'll be out in a minute."

"I want to show you something," he said. He took my hand and placed it over the hard mound of his crotch.

"Can you feel that?" he asked. "I've wanted you since the first day I first saw you." He put a hand on one breast. "I promise I will make you feel good."

Whether from my submissive personality in the face of his bravado or because unwittingly I felt my own need, I am ashamed to say I did nothing for several seconds. I won't blame it on the wine.

"Think about it," he said. "You won't be disappointed."

"Your wife is my friend," I thought to say. I didn't think to mention I was married, too.

"It happens all the time, Libby. Let me come over tomorrow. I'll watch for Cole's car to leave. You must know." His eyebrows bowed upward in a look of shameless expectation.

My breath caught, and I could only shake my head no. That it had taken this for the simple, stupid truth to dawn on me. That my marriage was transparent.

That I had become attractive as the lonely wife next door.

IN THE KITCHEN
by Ilana Stanger Ross

winner of the 2003 Flash in the Attic Contest

I entered the kitchen and found my father standing over the garbage can, grimacing, eating cheese.

"Your mother buys too much cheese," he said, his voice dry with the salt of it, "and then you, with your crazy diets, don't eat it and it goes bad and I have to eat it all."

"Dad," I said, with the easy smile of my privileged generation, "That cheese cost what, seven dollars? Less even. The money's gone whether it gets eaten or not, so you might as well just throw it away."

My father nodded as I spoke, leaving the cheese temporarily unmolested. "Yes," he said, "This is true. You're right, I don't need to eat this cheese." And with that he tossed the cheese, saran wrap and all, into the garbage.

I thought, Wow, look at that, I cured my father of the Great Depression.

We each ate a carrot in celebration.

But it didn't last. My father went back to his old ways, eating his cheese from between the mold. Once I even found him biting into a kitchen magnet. It was made to look like a cookie, and glazed, and it had slid from the refrigerator onto the floor, where my father saw it lying, just being wasted.

The dentist fixed his chipped tooth, said, "Well, these things happen."

I never gave my speech again, understood the futility. I knew my voice was clear and my father recognized its truth, but his mother's voice was louder in his ear, whispering, "Ess, ess mein kind, die kinder geyen aus fun hunger in Europe." Eat, eat my child, for in Europe the children are dying of hunger.

There are forty years between my father and me; there is so much we cannot explain to each other as we stand at separate ends of my mother's kitchen, eating.

CONTRIBUTORS

When **Neal Allen** (First Place for "Mayan Calendar) was laid off as a vice president of product development for a Fortune 20 company in 2011, he returned to writing. A short story was recently published in *The MacGuffin*. He has completed one novel and is working on a second. Single and helping his fourth child launch into adulthood, Neal lives in Orinda, California. He blogs about another passion, finding the transcendent in live music, at alivejive.blogspot.com. Neal is forever indebted to his studies at St. John's College, whose Great Books program lit up his pattern recognition hardware and illuminated a lifelong curiosity toward the sciences, philosophy, and human behavior. He also has an MA in Political Science from Columbia University.

Steve Almond ("Chibas Speaks") is the author of ten books, including the story collections *My Life in Heavy Metal, God Bless America, The Evil B.B. Chow and Other Stories*, and *This Brings Me to You* (co-authored with Julianna Baggott. His nonfiction books include

Candyfreak, Rock and Roll Will Save Your Life, and *Letters from People Who Hate Me*, among others. He lives in Massachusetts. Get the goods at stevealmondjoy.com. "Chibas Speaks" first appeared in issue 10 of *Ficiton Attic: The Journal of Elegant Wit*.

Andrew Blackman ("Pigs Are Intelligent") is a former *Wall Street Journal* writer, now living in London and concentrating on fiction. His second novel, *A Virtual Love* (Legend, 2013), tackles the theme of identity in the age of social media. His first novel, *On Holloway Road* (Legend, 2009), won the Luke Bitmead Writer's Bursary and was shortlisted for the Dundee International Book Prize. He blogs about writing and books at www.andrewblackman.net.

Mary Byrne ("Waiting for the Electricity") was born in Ireland and currently lives in France. She is a freelance French-English translator. Her short fiction has been published in or is forthcoming in Europe, North America, Australia, and included in anthologies such as *Best New Irish Short Stories* (Fabers, 2008), *Queens Noir* (Akashic, 2008), and *Best Paris Stories* (Summertime, 2012). She received the 2011 *Fiction International* Short Fiction Award 2011 and the 2012 Kore Press Short Fiction Award. Her chapbook *A parallel life* will be published by Kore Press in Fall 2013.

E.A. Fow is originally from New Zealand but lives and writes in Brooklyn, NY. She has an MFA from Brooklyn College, CUNY, and more of her work can be found at EAFow.com.

Anne Fox ("Choices") copyedits *Write Angles*, newsletter of the California Writers Club, Berkeley Branch. She co-copyedited the CWC Write On! story contest chapbook, and she copyedits for writers of fiction and nonfiction. Her writing has appeared in *Able Muse, Tiny Lights, The Sun, West Winds, Hippocampus Magazine* (December 2012), and the anthology, *Bacopa*, 2013, among others.

Patricia Friedrich ("When It Rains on Your Birthday") is an Associate Professor at Arizona State University. She is the editor of three books: *Language, Negotiation and Peace* (Continuum); *Teaching Academic Writing (Continuum);* and *Nonkilling Linguistics: Toward Practical Applications (*The Center for Global Nonkilling). Her fiction and nonfiction have appeared in *Harvard Business Review, World Englishes, Grey Sparrow, Eclectic Flash*, and *Blue Guitar,* among other journals. Her novel manuscript, *Artful Women,* won first prize at a Romance Writers of America regional competition (as a mainstream fiction entry). Find out more at patricia-friedrich.com.

Alan Gartenhaus contributed "Think of Me Babe Whenever" to this anthology. He lives in Hawaii.

Sharon Goldberg (runner up for "Rear-End Collisions") lives in the Seattle area and previously worked as an advertising copywriter in Los Angeles, San Francisco, and Seattle. Her work has appeared or is forthcoming in *The Louisville Review, Under the Sun, The Chaffey Review, Temenos, The Binnacle, Little Fiction: Listerature, The Feathered Flounder*, three fiction anthologies, and elsewhere. Her short stories "Caving In" (2012) and "Ghost" (2011) were finalists in the Pacific Northwest Writers Association Literary Contest. Sharon was also the second place winner of the 2012 *On The Premises* Humor Contest. She is working on a short story collection.

Vanessa Hua (Staking Claim) is an award-winning journalist and fiction writer. Her work has appeared in many newspapers, magazines, and anthologies, including *The Atlantic Monthly, ZYZZYVA, The New York Times,* and *Newsweek.* "Staking Claim" first appeared in issue 5 of *Fiction Attic: The Journal of Elegant Wit.*

By day, **Zachary Kaplan-Moss** ("A to B") is a farmer. By night, he is asleep. Throughout, he makes up stories short and long, a few of which can be found in the pages of *Zymbol, Cactus Heart, Alimentum,* and *Emprise Review.*

Hayley Kolding ("325") lives in a small Connecticut town where all sorts of stories happen. She works the counter and teaches flute lessons at a local music shop and spends plenty of time exploring the woods around town. She also plays the sax and is a student at Yale University. Most recently, Hayley's writing has been published in magazines of Susquehanna University and the University of Connecticut.

C.S. Kynehart ("Flying") is a California native who has published news articles for *The Campanil,* a newspaper affiliated with Mills College in Oakland,

California, where she earned a BA in English. Since graduating in 2010, she has been traveling cross-country and abroad as part of her work for a nonprofit. She recently finished writing a novel.

Ed Malone ("The New World") is a recent graduate of the NEOMFA program through Cleveland State University. He teaches college English and lives in Cleveland, Ohio.

R.F Marazas ("Stranger") won first place in the Dahlonega Literary Festival 2007 Novel Contest for Dimensions in Ego and has published short fiction and flash fiction in ten anthologies and online/print venues.

Corey Mesler has published in numerous journals and anthologies. He has published seven novels, most recently *Frank Comma and The Time-Slip* (2012), three full-length poetry collections, and three books of short stories, most recently *I'll Give You Something to Cry About* (2011). He has also published a dozen chapbooks of both poetry and prose. He has been nominated for the Pushcart Prize numerous times, and two of his poems were chosen for Garrison Keillor's Writer's Almanac. His fiction has received praise from John Grisham, Robert Olen Butler, Lee Smith, Frederick Barthelme, Greil Marcus, among others. With his wife, he runs Burke's Book Store in Memphis TN. He can be found at www.coreymesler.wordpress.com.

Clare Needham ("Black Onyx") graduated from Barnard College in 2008, and was a recent fellow at the MacDowell Colony. She is working on revisions of her first novel, and has recently finished a draft of her second. Her work has been published in *The New Inquiry* and *Armchair/Shotgun*, and was shortlisted for the Fish Publishing Prize. She edited and helped translate *Our Harsh Logic: Israeli Soldiers' Testimonies from the Occupied Territories, 2000-2010*, published by Metropolitan Books in 2012, and is currently editing *The Fires of Arno Stolz*, about the life of a German monk in Jerusalem during the Second World War.

Tim Norton ("Movement") first published a poem in a local poetry anthology while in college in 1999, followed by several other publications in successive years. He graduated with a BA in the Liberal Arts program at George Washington University with a minor in English and Creative Writing and was a student of Vikram Chandra, Tony Hoagland and David McAleavey. His relationship to language has been varied and turbulent at times. In order to supplement and placate his often tumultuous relationship to writing, he is working on getting an MS in Computer Science at the George Mason University in Northern Virginia as his other passion.

Meg Pokrass ("Shrine" and "Summer Gun") is the author of *Damn Sure Right* (Press 53), a collection of flash fiction. Her stories, essays, and poems have appeared in around 200 publications, including *The Rumpus, PANK, Nano Fiction, Smokelong Quarterly,*

Wigleaf, and *McSweeney's Internet Tendency,* among others. Meg's work was showcased for Dzanc Book's Short Story Month and nominated for Best of the Web, in addition to being nominated multiple times for The Pushcart Prize Anthology and chosen four years in a row for *Wigleaf's Top 50 [Very] Short Fictions.*

Robert Pope ("Shape Shifter," "The Lonesome Alien") is the author of the novel *Jack's Universe* and the story collection *Private Acts,* both from Another Chicago Press, as well as personal essays and short stories in many journals, most recently *Kenyon* Review, *Camera Obscura, New World Writing,* and a novella in the fall 2012 *Conium Review.* He teaches at The University of Akron, part of the Northeast Ohio MFA (NEOMFA).

S.J. Powers ("You and PJ and Molly and Zack" and "Like Nourishment") recently won first prize in New Millennium's Short Short Story Contest. Her stories have appeared in numerous publications, including *Another Chicago Magazine, SmokeLong Quarterly, StoryQuarterly,* and *SWELL.* She has received two Illinois Arts Council prizes and two of her stories have been nominated for the Pushcart Prize.

Michelle Richmond (editor) is the *New York Times* bestselling author of *The Year of Fog, No One You Know, Dream of the Blue Room,* the forthcoming novel *Golden State,* and the award-winning story collections *The Girl in the Fall-Away Dress* and *Hum.* She is the founder of Fiction Attic Press. http://michellerichmond.com.

Joshua Rigsby ("When It Burst") is a Los Angeles-based freelance writer and a stay-at-home dad. A former marketing director for North America's largest organic tea importer, Joshua is a certified tea specialist, and enjoys writing about the history and culture of tea. He has written dozens of articles for leading trade publications and magazines. His website, joshuarigsby.com, shares tips and strategies about scheduling, research, marketing, and the craft of writing for fulltime writer/parents.

JL Schneider ("Karliski Walks") is a carpenter and an adjunct professor of English at a small community college in upstate New York. His fiction has appeared in *Snake Nation, The Newport Review, The MacGuffin, International Quarterly, New Millennium Writings,* and *Onion River Review,* among others. His short story collection, *Objects of Desire,* was awarded the 2012 Sol Books Prose Prize.

Ilana Stanger-Ross ("In the Kitchen," winner of the 2003 Flash in the Attic contest) earned a Masters in Fiction from Temple University. Her critically acclaimed novel, *Sima's Undergarments for Women,* was published in 2008. She has received a Leeway Foundation Grant for Emerging Artists, as well as a residency grant from the Ragdale Foundation. Her stories have appeared in *Red Rock Review, The Bellevue Review,* and elsewhere. She currently lives with her husband and children in Victoria, BC, where she works as a Registered Midwife.

Bob Thurber ("Seaside Hitchhiker") worked at writing every day for twenty years before submitting his work. He went on to collect numerous awards and citations, including The Barry Hannah Fiction Prize and The Meridian Editors' Prize. Most recently he was a finalist in the 2012 Esquire/Aspen Writers' Foundation Short Fiction contest. His work has appeared in two dozen anthologies, and he is the author of *Paperboy: A Dysfunctional Novel* (Casperian Books, 2011) as well as a collection of exceedingly brief stories titled *Nickel Fictions*. For more info, visit his website http://www.bobthurber.net/

M. Kaat Toy (Katherine Toy Miller) ("Relinquishing Underwater Parallax Delirium") has completed a short story collection and three novels and published novel selections, short stories, flash fiction, prose poetry, and creative nonfiction. Her prose poem chapbook, *In a Cosmic Egg*, is available at Finishing Line Press. Her flash fiction book, *Disturbed Sleep*, is forthcoming from FutureCycle Press (www.futurecycle.org). She also does scholarly work on D. H. and Frieda Lawrence, Aldous Huxley, and Georgia O'Keeffe, mutual friends who lived briefly in Taos, New Mexico, which is her permanent residence. She will appear in a BBC documentary on Lawrence.

Eric Scot Tryon ("Supplemental Oxygen" and "My Sister Paula") lives in southern California where he teaches creative writing at Chapman University and Orange County School of the Arts. His work has previously appeared in *Glimmer Train*, *Willow Springs*, *Flash: The International Short-Short Story*

Magazine (UK), *Wisconsin Review, Rio Grande Review, Eureka Literary Magazine, Enigma Magazine,* and the anthology *Hunting Ghosts* (Black Oak Media, 2012).

Katy Whittingham ("Being Linda Marten") holds an MFA in Creative Writing from Emerson College, Boston. A poet, fiction writer, and photographer, her work has been published in numerous journals and magazines. Her collection, *By a Different Ocean,* was published by Plan B Press, Virginia in 2009. She teaches composition and creative writing at Bridgewater State University and the University of Massachusetts Dartmouth. Her other teaching and research interests include Irish American Studies, Children's Literature, and the incorporation of poetry in the early childhood classroom.

Susan Beckham Zurenda ("The Informant") has taught English for 33 years at Spartanburg Community College and Spartanburg High School. She is retiring from teaching this year to join Magic Time Literary Agency as a publicist. She is the winner of The Southern Writers Symposium Emerging Writers Fiction Contest and several other awards. With her two daughters grown, she lives with her husband Wayne and two Boston Terriers.

To read more great fiction,
and to submit your work,
please visit us online at
http://fictionattic.com